HARD-DRIVING EDGE

"One other thing, feller," Edge said before the Mexican could speak. "You gave your word to stick around so long as I stayed with the outfit. I figure a man who breaks his word ain't worth nothing more than a bullet."

Lacalle's anger broke surface as he whirled to glower at the calm, soft-spoken half-breed. "How can a man like you set store by honor?" he snarled. "A man who can cut the throat of another while holding a gun on him? . . ."

"I am what I am. And I ain't either proud or ashamed of it . . . anymore. You'll go all the way, feller," the half-breed said. "Or stay right here. As buzzard meat."

THE EDGE SERIES:

Best-Selling Series!

#27 The Most Violent Westerns in Print

EDGE

DEATH DRIVE

BY

George G. Gilman

PINNACLE BOOKS • LOS ANGELES

This is a work of fiction. All the characters and
events portrayed in this book are fictional,
and any resemblance to real people or incidents
is purely coincidental.

EDGE #27: DEATH DRIVE

Copyright © 1978 by George G. Gilman

All rights reserved, including the right to reproduce
this book or portions thereof in any form.

A Pinnacle Books edition, published by special
arrangement with New English Library,
Limited, London
First printing, September 1978
First published in Great Britain by
New English Library, Limited, 1978

ISBN: 0-523-40203-1

Cover illustration by Bruce Minney

Printed in the United States of America

PINNACLE BOOKS, INC.
2029 Century Park East
Los Angeles, California 90067

For C. E.

A new hand from
The Man
with No Name Territory

DEATH DRIVE

unicorns' herd?"

"S. Worth much money ... back life for the dead.

... it pays for terrible loss, feller." Billy ... Sally as he looked ... horse forward as

Chapter One

THE cantina smelled of bad cooking, spilled liquor, old tobacco smoke, the sweat of unwashed bodies and—strongest of all—the human waste rotting in the latrine out back. The midday heat that oozed in through the open front and rear doorways was absorbed by the malodorous atmosphere trapped between the adobe walls and added to it yet another pungent stench: that of three thousand head of cattle penned in the stockyards on the east side of town.

One of the trio of men who stepped out of the harsh glare of sunlight into the rancid shade showed no response to the evil odors, which at once assaulted his nostrils. While the two who trailed him grimaced—almost as if their sense of smell triggered a stab of pain—and pulled up short on the threshold.

"Christ Almighty, Barney, this place reeks worse than a sewer!"

He was the oldest of the three, close to sixty with graying and thinning hair that produced enough dandruff to sprinkle his shoulders like snow. He was short and heavily built, his weight problem caused by the ravages of good living. His face was round with soft, curved features. In younger years, perhaps they had been angular, which would have made him handsome. Today, though, he was merely a short, fat man moving ungracefully out of middle toward old age.

"And it's hotter than hell itself!"

1

The man who rasped this and waved a hand vigorously in front of his face was in his late twenties—a younger, taller and leaner version of the first speaker. Leaner only because he was six feet tall, so that the fat of overindulgence was more evenly distributed on his frame. His hair was black and thicker, slicked down across the head in the same neatly clipped style as that of his father. He was good looking in a weak, almost characterless way: for already his face had fleshed out to conceal the bone structure.

Both men had green eyes that emanated disdain with the ease of long experience. Both had complexions of painful red from being exposed to strong sunlight after a long time of living beyond the reach of the elements. Both wore Western outfits of riding boots, Levis, checked shirts, kerchiefs and Stetsons: every item of their apparel stiff with store-bought newness except where patches of sweat staining showed.

"Then I figure we've come to the right place," Barney answered, his Texas drawl sounding very pronounced after the cultured, Eastern accents of the other two. "On account that sewer rats and hellions are the only kinda guys we're likely to get to work for us."

He had come to a halt just inside the cantina and, as he spoke, without looking back at the doorway, he displayed an expression of disgust. But it was obviously his reaction to the occupants of the place rather than to any aspect of their surroundings. He, too, was dressed in workaday Western clothes; but it was a long time since they had been new and he had done a great deal of hard work in them. He carried a battered leather valise.

He was forty and matched the older man's height of five feet six inches. But there was no excess fat on his broad shoulders and wide chest. His shirt and Levis clung tight to solid, muscular flesh. The skin, which was stretched taut over the bones of his face, was dark

2

brown, scarred deep by lines from exposure to the harsher side of life. His teeth were also brown, staining heavier by the moment as he chewed a wad of tobacco. His eyes were coal black, dulled by sourness, as he raked them over the squalid scene in front of him.

Buenas tardes, Americanos! You wanna drink to make the day not seem so hot, uh? You come to the best place in town. We serve only the best!"

"To the worst people, looks like," Barney snarled in response to the cheerful greeting of the beaming bartender.

The fat, leather-aproned, middle-aged man simply gave a shrug of resignation and assumed his former look of concentration as he watched the mating antics of two roaches on the floor between his bare feet. Everyone else in the cantina appeared equally unmoved by Barney's insult.

A dozen of the customers were Mexicans, aged from ten to eighty. A boy was seated on the floor by a door that opened to the kitchen. After it became obvious the newcomers did not want food, he resumed his study of a man across the room from where he sat. An old-timer held an almost empty beer glass and stared morosely at the flat dregs in the bottom, wanting desperately to drink but deterred by the prospect of having none left at all. The rest were *vaqueros.* Five slept, perhaps drunk or maybe merely weary of the heat; all snored. Four more played a card game without stakes while another watched. All these had empty shot glasses close at hand and there was a pot of salt in the center of their table.

The man who was watched by the boy was not a Mexican. Although there was certainly a look of the Latin about him, Barney and the other two newcomers noted, when he tilted his hat up from his face and eyed the doorway bleakly.

"You got a bad mouth, feller," he said lazily and

3

there was no trace of Mexican in his accent. Rather, his voice placed his origins in the Midwest.

Barney's scowl deepened as he glanced away from the American to make a second survey of the other customers. "I'm known for it, mister," he rasped. "But there's good money waitin' for men willin' to listen to it from here to Laramie."

The card game came to an abrupt end. The nonplayer woke up one of the sleeping men and nodded toward Barney. *"Dinero!"* he said sharply.

And the other instantly jerked out of sleep. They were disoriented for a moment, but then realized their attention should be focused on the three men in the doorway. The bartender continued to study the roaches, the old-timer to stare into his near empty glass and the boy to watch the American who so obviously had some Mexican blood in his veins. This man remained slumped low in a chair with arms, far enough back from a table so that he could rest his feet comfortably on its top. Ever since he had pushed his hat off his face and onto his head as he responded to Barney, he had been slowly rolling a cigarette. His elbows were braced on the stock and barrel of a Winchester rifle that rested on the chair arms.

"Just for listening, feller?" he asked after licking the gummed edge of the paper.

Barney vented a wet grunt of irritation at the interruption, which came just as he was gaining the attention of his audience. He spat a stream of brown tobacco juice to the floor. "For drivin' a herd of prime longhorns. You'll get the bad mouth every time you screw up what I'll tell you to do. And if you ain't interested, mister, best you shut up so as I can talk to men who are."

He looked briefly at the Mexican-American again, but saw little of the face through the cloud of expelled tobacco smoke from the newly lit cigarette.

4

"Go ahead, feller. But the only mistake that's been made so far was by you. So best you keep it polite from here on in."

It was apparent that Barney was a man with a short temper. But he managed to contain an impulse to show it and merely sighed before replying—his dull, dark eyes swinging across the eagerly interested faces of the Mexicans. "From here on into Laramie, Mr. Taggart is ready to pay a hundred bucks a man a week. That sound polite enough for you, mister?"

Several of the Mexicans gasped their surprise, then blurted out their excitement to each other. Barney, still sullen, shifted his dull-eyed gaze to the man with his feet up on the table. The cigarette had been lowered from the mouth now and he saw the man's face clearly for the first time.

"It sounds like a lot of money for the worst, feller," the man answered as the Mexicans quieted.

The elder of the Easterners cleared his throat as, like Barney, he did a double take and realized he had received a wrong first impression of the man with the Winchester. "It's the kind of day that encourages bad tempers, sir," he said with an attempt at a placating smile. "And I'm afraid Mr. Tait is not the most tactful of men at the best of times. If you would care to . . ."

"Come on, Dad!" his son cut in irritably, batting his hand more vigorously in front of his face. "Let's leave Barney to sign up those that want to work for us. At the rates we're paying, we don't have to beg."

The father regarded his son with scornful patience, then sighed as he returned his attention to the man lounging in the chair across the cantina. "Ezekiel is also inclined to be rather quarrelsome in this awful heat," he offered apologetically. "And I have to admit that I have difficulty in abiding by the civilities on occasions."

He licked his lips, anxious that his apology should

5

be accepted. His son was still petulant. Barney Tait was enduring a slow burning feeling, uncomfortably conscious that there was a more important reason than the presence of his boss, which forced him to keep his feelings under control.

"It figures you people are always looking to pick fights," the man allowed evenly as he swung his feet down from the table and eased lazily upright from the chair. Then he canted the Winchester to his right shoulder and curled back his lips to show a quiet grin in response to the quizzical looks directed at him. "Seeing as how you're in the beef business."

The boy laughed. "That was very funny, *señor!*" he called as the man moved between tables and chairs to approach the doorway to the street.

Others, with the exception of the preoccupied bartender and the old Mexican contemplating his glass, reacted to the abrupt lessening of tension without words or even smiles. While Ezekiel Taggart, directly in the path of the man nearing the door, only now became aware of a feeling much stronger than mere discomfort in the heat and stink of the cantina. And he swallowed hard as he side-stepped to leave the exit clear.

Just as others had been a few moments before, the young Easterner attired in his brand new Western garb was receiving a seond impression of the man. And what he saw triggered an unnerving sense of dread in his mind.

The man moving across the evil-smelling cantina in a loose-limbed, casual gait was exceptionally tall— three inches above six feet. He was at once heavy, yet lean, his two hundred pounds moulded in blatantly masculine proportions to his lanky frame. It was the physique of a superbly fit man in his mid to late thirties, providing an odd contrast with his face, which seemed to be that of a man several years older. It was

6

a long, lean face with clearly defined features, most prominent of which were the eyes—light blue and piercing, permanently narrowed beneath hooded lids. The nose, flanked by high cheekbones, had a hawklike quality. The lips were long and thin above a firm, jutting jaw. His skin was dark brown, deeply inscribed with the furrows of the passing years. The hair, which fell from under the brim of his hat to touch his shoulders and top of his back, was jet black.

His dress was subdued and lacked affectation. A straw sombrero and black denim pants. A gray shirt and kerchief. Spurless riding boots. Around his waist, a gunbelt with a low-slung holster tied down to the thigh. There was a Remington revolver in the holster and spare shells were slotted into every loop of the belt.

All this could be seen in a first, indifferent glance at the man. It might also be noted that, when he was freshly shaved, he wore a mustache, for the bristles of more than forty-eight hours sprouted longer and thicker above his top lip and around the sides of his mouth down onto his jaw. And the more perceptive were also likely to discern clues to his mixed blood— the color of his hair and skin inherited from a Latin parent while the blueness of his eyes was undoubtedly drawn from a northern European heritage. The rest of his features were the result of a harmonious amalgam of the two bloodlines.

The whole was perhaps handsome, perhaps forbidding—depending upon how one responded to latent cruelty and a capacity to meet evil with like. Behind the veneer of calm nonchalance these qualities of the man's character were easily seen by anybody who chose to study him with more than mild interest.

The Mexicans in the cantina had all seen this before the three newcomers appeared. But only the young boy who waited on tables had sensed something about the lone American that was more deeply concealed.

7

Barney Tait and the elder Taggart had also recognized early the subtle signs—visible in the cold blue eyes and set of the thin lips—that this was a man different to most others.

Now the other Taggart received a true impression of the man, and the sweat standing out on his sun-reddened face and staining his new clothes felt suddenly icy—as if frozen by the cold power that came from the glinting eyes.

"You're not interested in a job then?" he asked hurriedly, no longer stirring the hot, stinking air in front of his face.

"Sure I'm interested, feller. But for a hundred dollars a week I figure I'd have to know more about beef than that I like my steaks well done."

Then he was gone, stepping across the threshold and out onto the broad, dusty street under the harsh glare of early afternoon sun. Taking in a deep breath through flared nostrils but smelling only cows and woodsmoke—failing to draw any hint of freshness from the three-hundred-foot-wide Rio Grande that flowed sluggishly past the back lots of the buildings across the street.

"Man, that's one mean sonofabitch!" Barney Tait rasped through tightly clenched teeth as soon as the footfalls of the man had receded from earshot.

"You won't ever say anything truer than that, Mr. Tait," Ezekiel Taggart murmured, and took his hat from where it hung down his back, to use it for a fan as his sweat lost its icy feel.

His father ignored both men to survey the eager Mexicans with distaste. "Anybody here know who that man is?" he demanded, his tone harsh with authority.

There were shrugs and blank faces. Then the young boy rose to speak, but the bartender replied first, as he dropped a bare heel on the roaches and ground them to a pulp against the dirt floor.

8

"The *Americano,* he come to town this morning, *señor.* He had only *dinero* for one tortilla and beer. He says little. Sleeps or maybe does not sleep until you come."

He had finished and he lifted his foot to study the pulp that had once been a pair of mating roaches.

"He is one sad *hombre, señors,*" the boy added with a frown and in a melancholy tone. "When I say, why is this? he tells me I remind him of somebody."

The elder Taggart shook his head, dissatisfied with the information. Then he swept a hand across the front of his body to encompass the cantina. "If this is the best we can get, sign up all those who want a job, Barney," he instructed tersely. "I've got business elsewhere."

He spun on his heels and strode outside, reaching over his shoulders to grasp his hat and jam it hard on his head. His son hurried to catch up with him.

"What business, Dad?" he asked wearily, eyeing the whole length of the hot, dusty, squalid street with grim distaste.

"Hiring him, boy!" his father growled resolutely, pointing a pudgy finger out of a tight fist toward the familiar tall man leading a horse from a stable. Ezekiel opened his mouth to protest, but his father abruptly stepped away from him and shouted, "Hey, you there! I have a proposition for you!"

The man had swung up into the saddle of his black gelding, not sliding the rifle into its boot until he was mounted. There was nobody else on the street and when he had ridden his horse across to where the Taggarts stood they formed a close knit group in a seemingly deserted world.

The rider looked down at the two red-faced men, his eyes glinting slits of blue under the shade of the sombrero brim. The butt of his almost smoked cigarette was angled at the corner of his thin mouth.

9

"I hear you're broke." Taggart said, having to struggle against the impulse to resent the mounted man's tacit arrogance.

"Bad news always travels fast," came the even-voiced reply.

"A hundred and fifty dollars a week. And you don't have to know a thing about herding cows. Just how to keep men from trying to stop the drive north."

The final quarter inch of cigarette was taken from the corner of the mouth and flicked into the center of the street. "For a week's pay in advance, you've got yourself a trouble-shooter, feller."

The father smiled and the son grimaced.

"You sure, Dad? Tait might not like it."

"Barney Tait's only foreman of the Bit-T," the older Taggart said, his face still tilted up toward the mounted man. "I own it. Consider yourself hired, mister!"

A brown-skinned hand released the reins and was extended, palm upwards.

"Tait's in charge of the payroll. Tell him I've agreed your terms." His sun-punished overindulged face showed the start of an anxious frown. "Try to stay on good terms with him. I need him more than I . . . Hey, where do you think you're going?"

The man had withdrawn his hand and heeled his horse forward. Just a few yards, to the hitching rail outside the cantina. Taggart's resentment rose to the surface and altered the lines of his frown into an angry snarl.

"You just made a deal with a real hungry feller," came the soft-spoken reply as the rider swung down from his saddle and hitched the reins to the rail.

"We heard you could only afford a tortilla for breakfast," Ezekiel taunted, relishing the tall man's destitution as some kind of minor triumph.

"It didn't do much to fill a three-day hole."

"All right," the elder man allowed, and chided his

10

son with a brief glower. "Just keep in mind what I told you about Barney Tait. I need you, mister. But I don't want you coming between me and my foreman just because . . ."

"Don't aim to cause no trouble between you and him, feller," the tall, lean man interrupted evenly. And he smiled in the same way he had done in the cantina—drawing back his thin lips to display his very white teeth, without injecting even part of a degree of warmth into his gaze. "But if he don't hand over some eating money soon, I could get to be the thin Edge of the wedge."

Chapter Two

THE malodorous cantina was doing good business as the man called Edge retraced his steps among the scattered tables and sat down in the same chair he had used before. Only the boy—who came away from the kitchen doorway in response to the half-breed's crooked forefinger—and Barney Tait, paid him any attention.

"Two more tortillas, bowl of chili and a whole pot of coffee."

"You have money now, *señor?*" the boy asked, surprised. And shot an anxious glance over his shoulder toward the bartender.

The aproned man was busy pouring tequila for newly rich *vaqueros*, while the final few applicants for jobs on the cattle drive stood impatiently in line at a table where Tait sat, the battered valise open in front of him.

"Will have by the time you give me the check," Edge answered, impassive in the face of irritably puzzled glances that Tait cast toward him.

"*Si, señor*. I trust you."

The boy scuttled away, hurrying to reach the cover of the kitchen before the avariciously busy bartender saw him.

Edge watched the last man on the line do business with Tait. It was the old-timer, who did not gulp the dregs of his beer until he had scrawled his name on a sheet of paper and been rewarded with a stack of bills from the valise. Then, as the elderly Mexican moved with unsteady haste toward the bar, Tait rose from his chair, stuffed the much signed contract into the valise and snapped close the clasps. He looked long and hard at Edge, seemed about to swing toward the crowded bar, but abruptly changed his mind. The scowl on his face was firmly set when he halted at the half-breed's table.

"You just take some fast lessons in handlin' beef on the hoof, mister?" he growled.

Edge stretched out a long leg beneath the table to push a chair against the front of Tait's legs. "It's still all just raw meat to me, feller," he answered evenly.

Tait's scowl began to expand toward a snarl of rage. But then he sighed, dropped into the offered chair and opened the valise. "How much the old man payin' to hire your gun, mister?"

"One fifty a week. Just the one week in advance."

Fully resigned to the situation now, Tait pulled the contract from his valise and pushed it across the scarred table top. Then he delved into a pocket of his shirt to produce a pencil stub. "Tell you what I told the greasers, mister. The Big-T spread's ten miles northwest of here. Five thousand head have been rounded up and penned ready to move. They'll move at dawn tomorrow. And nobody'll get another cent until them beeves reach Laramie."

The boy emerged from the kitchen, the opening of the door wafting in a new aroma of freshly cooked food. The youngster carried a smoke blackened coffee pot and a mug. The bartender saw him and his greedy grin was suddenly gone, replaced by an angry glower as he realized the order was for Edge. But his gaze found the half-breed just as the previously broke man traded a sheet of paper for a stack of bills. The boy saw the grin return and was happy himself, like everybody else in the cantina except for the two seated Americans.

"One other thing . . ." Tait drawled, glancing at the crumpled and grease marked contract ". . . Edge?"

"That's the right name, feller," was the quiet-voiced reply as the boy set down the coffee pot and mug. "Obliged, kid."

"The Taggarts will be ridin' with us but I reckon they know less about cows than you do. The old man hired you and that's his money in your hip pocket. But from the spread to Laramie, I'll be boss. You'll do what I tell you, when I tell you. And the way I tell you, if that's the way it has to be."

His soured eyes stared hard into Edge's face, challenging him to contest this rule.

"Always respect a man who knows more than I do, feller," the half-breed allowed, tilting the spout of the coffee pot over the mug.

Tait nodded curtly and reclosed the valise. He started to rise from the chair as two more Mexicans swung into the cantina from the street—their presence abruptly curtailing the excited talk and happy laughter of the group gathered at the bar. Intrigued by the sudden end to the din, Tait turned his head. He was half out of his chair, body tilted forward. A grunt of alarm burst from his throat as a brown-skinned hand grabbed his kerchief and jerked him hard across the table.

He dropped the valise and gripped the table with one hand, the other clenching for a defensive blow as his flailing feet were dragged up off the floor. But then, when he was sprawled across the table top, one bristled cheek pressed hard to the back of Edge's left wrist, he became terrified into stillness. For his dark eyes, the lids wide and the irises swiveled to their fullest extent, saw the half-breed's capacity for evil was no longer latent. And he saw that his right hand grasped a vicious instrument of torture and death.

14

Tait saw the other man's eyes as the merest threads of glinting blueness, while the lips were compressed so tightly that they seemed not to exist. The skin of the face was pulled drum taut between the bones, yet the lines of harshly lived years appeared more deeply inscribed.

In the right hand, which swung in a blur of speed from out of the thick hair at the nape of his neck, Edge held an open straight razor, the point honed as sharply as the cutting side. And it was the point which rested against the exposed side of Tait's pulsing throat.

The attack and capture had taken no more than two seconds and in that brief segment of time the newcomers on the threshold had been forgotten. Every pair of Mexican eyes was focused on the two Americans.

"No man knows everything, feller," Edge rasped into the hot, stinking silence. His lips moved only slightly, his teeth not at all. "So listen and learn. I hear you call Mexicans greasers again, I'll cut out your lousy tongue and make you swallow it whole. You got that, boss?"

"Let me up!" Tait snarled. But he did not struggle, his eyes switching their terrified gaze from the grim face of Edge to the razor which pricked his skin without drawing blood.

"You'll remember?" the half-breed insisted, his tone no longer so harsh.

"Sure! Sure! I didn't figure you for such a touchy bastard!"

"I ain't, feller. Except in two ways. And you and the rest of these people might as well know about the other thing that upsets me." He continued to keep a tight grip on Tait's kerchief and the razor against the skin as he raked his narrow-eyed gaze over the recently hired Big-T hands. The fear that the hard-set lines of his face had inspired in Barney Tait was now transmitted to the Mexicans. "Any man ever has cause to pull a

15

gun on me better squeeze the trigger right away. If he's lucky, he'll kill me. If he don't, he'll have a long stop-over someplace between here and Laramie. On account he'll be dead. Always try to give folks a warning."

He withdrew the razor from Tait's neck and pushed it, still open, into a leather pouch at the nape of his own neck—the sheath for the awesome weapon held in place by a beaded thong encircling his throat. Then he released his grip on the kerchief and picked up the mug of coffee. He sipped the strong liquid with quiet relish and his face became impassive in repose. He adopted the easy attitude without effort and it was as if no threat of violence had ever arisen.

"You men, we leave now!" one of the two new-comers snapped in Spanish.

Both of them were in their early thirties. Tall and lean and possessing Latin good looks. They were well and expensively attired in trail herding outfits, complete with *chaparejos* and spurs. Each carried a bone-handled Colt in a low, loose hanging holster.

The men who had just signed a contract to work for the Big-T looked sheepishly at each other. Some shuffled their feet.

Barney Tait, still disconcerted by the speed and icy coldness of Edge's anger and actions, took several moments to adjust to the new atmosphere that pervaded the cantina.

"You need me to teach you some Spanish, feller?" the half-breed asked softly as the two men on the threshold sensed trouble that involved them.

The Texan had dropped back into his chair. "No, I friggin' don't!" he snarled, springing erect and swinging around, rising anger jutting his jaw and setting light to his dark eyes. "What the hell's goin' on here?" he demanded in English.

His head swung from the men at the bar to those at the doorway and back again.

16

The old-timer spoke, but not to Tait. "We no longer work for you," he told the newcomers. "We will get much more money to take American beef to Laramie."

He looked less afraid than the men flanking him, perhaps because he was much older than all of them and therefore had less life left to lose. And his words certainly spread murderous looks across the faces of the men at the doorway. Some of the *vaqueros* nodded in shame-faced confirmation of what had been said. They were treated to scornful stares, which were then directed with deepening emotion toward Edge and Tait.

"You are Taggart men?" the taller of the two asked in English, making each word sound like an obscenity.

"Ain't no business of yours who we are, mister!" Tait snarled.

Both well-dressed Mexicans nodded.

"*Si*, that is what you are!" the thicker-set one flung at the Americans. "The scum of Texas who no *Americanos* will work for!" He snapped his head around to show the full measure of his contemptuous scowl to the *vaqueros*. "I hope they paid you well, you *loco hombres!* But whatever it was, it will not be enough! Even for your worthless lives!"

"You finished, mister?" Tait snarled.

"No, we have not finished, *señor*," the taller Mexican answered, moderating his tone and bringing his impulsive rage under control. He waved an arm to encompass the men at the bar. "They have worked for my brother and I a long time. We owe it to them to warn them of what will happen if they . . ."

"Ain't no 'if' about it." Tait cut in and dropped his right hand to drape the Colt in his holster. "They put their names to a contract and they got Taggart dollars in their pokes! So best you *hombres* leave. Before I maybe pay you out. For callin' me Texas scum."

Neither brother was perturbed by Tait's threats. Instead, their resolve became firmer. Their stances became less rigid and all traces of any emotion drained from their faces.

"*Señor* Tait!" the old-timer called anxiously. "Don Camilo and Don Jorge are known as the . . ."

"Best guns in the whole of Nuevo Leon state," Edge cut in, his tone commonplace in stark contrast to the old man's dramatic whisper. "If they're the Quinteros."

"*Si*, we are the Quinteros," the taller brother confirmed. He spoke the name with pride. "So I think we may be allowed to speak with our men . . ." He paused. "Without need to force the issue?"

The implied threat was much stronger than the stocky Texan's bluster had been. And its effect was much more dramatic. It excluded the *vaqueros* and the old-timer who became absorbed, natural spectators. Their blank faces turned toward Tait and heightened the Texan's new fear of the situation he had triggered off.

"You gonna start earnin' what you been paid, Edge?" Tait rasped from the corner of his mouth, his worried eyes moving only to flick between the faces of the Quinteros.

"You ain't got four feet and horns, feller," the half-breed countered evenly.

"Do you think a *gringo pistolero* frightens Don Jorge and I?" the taller brother taunted.

The door from the kitchen swung open, ushering in a stronger aroma of cooking as the boy emerged, a tray of steaming food balanced on one hand.

"Your meal, *señor!*" he called brightly, venting a sound that was half gasp, half cry of alarm.

Both Quintero brothers were distracted by the youngster's sudden and cheerful entrance and Barney Tait grunted his pleasure at this as he drew and cocked his Colt. But the exclamation finished as a sound of fear. For the two men at the doorway saw the Texan's move in the periphery of their vision. And combated it with the smooth skill of long experience. They drew their revolvers in perfect unison, at the same time side-stepping away from each other. It was inevitable that Tait, although he had the drop, should hesitate, torn between two targets.

"Crazy bastard!" Edge accused through clenched teeth. He jerked up both knees against the underside of the table.

The table tilted and went forward, slamming into Tait's back. The Texan bellowed a roar of pain and crashed to the floor. His gun was triggered into a wild shot that buried the bullet into the ceiling. The reports of the Quinteros' revolvers sounded simultaneously a fraction of a second later. Their shots were carefully aimed, but at a target that had abruptly fallen under the line of fire.

One bullet ricocheted off the flying, liquid-spilling coffee pot. The second exploded wood splinters from the table top as it became lodged in the tilted surface.

Edge had powered up from his chair and lunged to the side after overturning the table. The Remington—given to him by a Mexican boy much like the one now rooted to the threshold of the kitchen doorway—came clear of the holster as part of the same series of smooth movements.

Its first shot killed the brother named Don Camilo, drilling through his fancy vest to bore a hole in his heart. The impact of the bullet started him into a turn, but his legs went limp before it was half completed. And he crumpled to the floor like something wet and loosely packed. A final pumping action of his heart spurted liquid crimson across his chest.

Don Jorge had cocked his bone-handled revolver by then. But he was not a cold-hearted, feelingless loner like the man in a half crouch across the cantina from him. He was used to drawing confidence from the

19

knowledge - that he had a brother at his side. And the fact that his brother was now just a dead thing on the floor aroused a turmoil of emotions in his mind. He felt grief and anger, a need to confirm his worst fear and a thirst for revenge when he was forced to accept the inevitable truth.

But he was a skilled gunfighter, aware that he was in a kill-or-be-killed conflict. And it took him just a split-second to push all other considerations aside and concentrate on the immediate necessity.

A split-second was too long.

Edge felt nothing—neither that he had just killed a man, nor that he might himself be blasted into death by a bullet tunneling through his flesh. If he was aware of anything in his mind at all, it was simply a fleeting notion that he had the advantage—one brother could not witness the violent end of another without experiencing some kind of hindering emotion.

He squeezed the trigger of the Remington a second time and saw the Mexican's gun buck as it echoed the shot. But Don Jorge was already starting his backward stagger and the recoil of the revolver in the hand of a dead man jerked it farther off target. The bullet burrowed into dirt at the angle of a side wall and floor. It was a corpse which banged into the doorframe and pitched forward. Killed by another shot in the heart, marked by a black hole at the center of a blossoming crimson stain. He fell face down and remained that way, hiding from shocked and indifferent onlookers the expression of injured pride that was his death mask. A rivulet of blood from his punctured heart wound out from beneath his body to be soaked up by the dirt of the cantina floor.

"Dammit, I could've handled one of 'em!" Tait snarled, pushing up on to all fours and then coming erect. He grimaced and massaged the small of his back where the table had hit him. But then, after a glance at

20

the crumpled and sprawled corpses, he showed the half-breed his discolored teeth in a broad grin of relief. "Or maybe I couldn't have."

Edge upended the Remington to eject the two spent shell cases. He fed live rounds into the smoke-smelling chambers of the cylinder. "Every man to his trade, feller."

"*Niño!*" the bartender yelled at the still frightened boy. "Go bring the *Federales!*"

The boy was startled out of his horrified study of the crumpled and sprawled corpses. He looked anxiously around for a place to set down the tray of food. And saw the half-breed's outstretched hands.

"Obliged," Edge told him, and sat down at the nearest table as the youngster ran out of the rear door.

"Guess that's what I oughta say to you," Tait offered, looking and sounding awkward. "Thanks."

"Just doing the job I'm paid for, feller," the half-breed replied, as he dipped a tortilla into the chili bowl and began to eat.

"Even though I ain't got four legs and horns?" He retrieved the valise from beside the overturned table.

"That's just a matter of how you look," came the even voiced reply. "Inside you're just as full of bull-shit."

Tait was again quick to check an angry impulse. And he signaled his success with a shrug. "I already told you I'm known for my bad mouth. There's some things a man just can't help bein'."

"Like cold as a Sierra Madre night, *señor?*" the old-timer said mournfully, as shouts sounded out on the dusty street. He looked directly across the cantina at the contentedly chewing half-breed who met his doleful gaze with a look of mild curiosity. "In one minute you shoot the life of two men. I watch your face as you do this and you show no more feeling than if you are wringing the necks of two chickens. And the next minute, with the dead still warm at your feet, you can eat food. How can a man be so indifferent to such a . . ."

"Takes practice, old man," Edge answered around a mouthful of chili-dipped tortilla.

"And a willingness to learn, I think, *señor*."

A dispassionate nod. "That, too."

A fat *Federale* with triple chevrons on his sleeves appeared at the street doorway, sweat beads dropping off the curve of his jaw to splash new stains onto his uniform tunic. "What is going on here?" he demanded, a hand on his holstered revolver.

The boy was at his side and the Taggart father and son were behind him.

"A heart to heart talk," Edge replied, halting on the point of biting into the second tortilla. He stabbed it at his chest, then turned it toward the dead men who had now ceased to spill their blood. "Seems the old man figures mine shouldn't be empty when theirs are overflowing."

Chapter Three

THE tall, lean half-breed ate his meal and drank three mugs of coffee from a fresh pot delivered by the boy while everyone else in the cantina competed to tell the *Federale* non-com how the Quintero brothers came to die. For a few moments, he listened to the babble of voices, until old man Taggart yelled across the noise to command silence and the harassed sergeant was able to question witnesses and hear their individual responses clearly.

But Edge had already discerned enough from the initial babble of shouts to know that the *Federale* would cause him no trouble. Everyone would tell of the killing shots being fired in self-defense.

Edge himself was not certain whether this was the truth, but the implications of what might have been were of no concern to him. He had received payment in advance to see that a herd of Texas longhorns reached its destination in Laramie. And without an experienced trail boss to head up the newly formed outfit, such a drive would have been doomed from the start. So, to rescue Barney Tait from a deadly situation of his own making, Edge had gunned down two men.

As far as he was concerned, the incident was closed, unless others chose to make an issue of it.

The man who was now called Edge had not always regarded life and death in such a cold-bloodedly brutal manner. Once, long ago, when he had been Josiah C.

Hedges living with his close-knit family on their farmstead in Iowa, he had been no worse than many young men of his own age and better than many others.

Life had been hard but good and when the evil of violence and tragedy touched him, his responses were involuntarily drawn from the full gamut of human emotions.

Thus had he suffered intense anguish when a gun he was holding accidentally fired to explode a bullet into the leg of Jamie, his younger brother—to make the boy a cripple for the remainder of his short life.

But even then, so far back in time, the man who now sat in the stinking cantina of a Mexican town— poker-faced and totally dispassionate after killing two fellow human beings—had begun to learn the lessons of survival amid the dangers of the trade he was to adopt. For it was the shooting of Jamie that had sown the seed of his aversion to aimed guns. And, in retrospect, he had later realized he was defenseless while he endured the torment of seeing Jamie's agony. Thus had he been conscious of his advantage over one of the Quintero brothers while the other was still a warm corpse.

His Mexican father and Scandinavian mother were dead before the start of the War Between the States and his reaction to their dying had been less dramatic than he expected. But he understood this. It was more important to face the future than to dwell on the past, to tend the farm his parents had worked so hard to establish, and to provide for the lame Jamie. His responsibilities allowed little time for the luxury of grief. And such an attitude, which ruled almost every decision he took, served to temper his strength of character, just as the long and heavy farm work developed his physical powers.

When civil war came, he regarded it a responsible

decision to fight for the cause of the Union against a Confederacy that both he and Jamie considered a potent threat to the Hedges' way of life. But whatever had motivated his choice, the consequences of him making it were destined to work traumatic changes in almost every facet of the man now called Edge.

"*Señor* Edge, you can confirm everything that has been said by these men?" the *Federale* sergeant demanded officiously.

He had not questioned all of them—content to hear the matching accounts of the old-timer and the bartender, augmented by the many nods of agreement from Barney Tait and the *vaqueros*.

The half-breed completed lighting a cigarette and blew out a stream of smoke. "It was the Quinteros or Tait and me, feller," he replied evenly.

"You are a professional gunfighter?" He showed a scowl of contempt on his round, sweating face as he said this.

"I'm whatever I have to be to eat."

"Then I ask you to be this thing outside of this town, *señor*. It is a poor town, of people unfamiliar with the richness of much money." Now he directed his scorn toward the *vaqueros* and swung his head to include the trio of Tait and the Taggarts grouped close to the stiffening corpses. "You have achieved what you came here for. Take it and leave."

The *vaqueros* appeared suitably chastened, while the bartender responded to the *Federale*'s scorn with a sneer of his own.

"The *Americanos* have a saying, *Sargento*," he muttered. "That it is wrong to look the gift horse in the mouth."

"I can see why you approve such a sentiment," the *Federale* growled. "Which is why I will remain here until your son brings the undertaker. So that you will have no opportunity to rob the gift of corpses you have

25

had given to your filthy establishment. He pointed to the boy. "Go, *niño!*"

"And we're leavin', too!" Tait snapped at the *vaqueros* after the elder Taggart and whispered in his ear. "Get your horses and gear and meet us at the ford."

The bartender's sullen mood was abruptly matched by the men's, most of whom had empty glasses and no prospect of having them refilled.

"And bear this in mind!" Tait added, his voice louder and harsher to cut across the mumbling of discontent. "Any of you figured to take his advance and not show up, the Big-T outfit has a way of takin' care of that."

He looked meaningfully at the corpses, then switched his gaze toward Edge as the half-breed stifled the fire of his cigarette ash in the greasy chili bowl. The *Federale* saw that Edge, who got slowly to his feet, engendered a kind of awe among the *vaqueros* and he smiled cynically.

"It is to be hoped, *señor*," he said grimly, "that your enemies fear you more than your friends."

The half-breed shook his head. "I don't have any enemies, feller. That ain't dead."

"Nor friends, either," the old-timer put in sadly, and now had no hesitation in finishing his half-full glass of beer at a single swallow. "Just people who need him, I think."

Edge peeled a dollar off his new roll and dropped it on the table as a wagon jolted to a dust-raising halt on the street outside.

"Is too much, *señor!*" the boy called as he entered the cantina, drawing an angry scowl from his leather-aproned father.

"Keep the change, kid," the half-breed replied as he headed for the door. "A tip, and here's another one. In

26

my book, friends ain't worth the paper they're written on."

The puzzled youngster, who reminded him so strongly of another boy, stepped away from the threshold and Edge went out into the harsh sunlight. A tall and thin Mexican, strangely attired in white shirt and pants with a black necktie and stovepipe hat, was struggling to slide two pine coffins over the tail gate of the flatbed wagon.

"Is it true, *señor?*" he asked breathlessly. "What the boy has said? That Don Jorge and Don Camilo Quintero have been killed?"

"The story's true," Edge confirmed as he unhitched the reins of the gelding from the rail. "It's a couple of characters who are starting to smell."

The undertaker looked affronted. "I got here as fast as I could, *señor.*"

"No sweat, feller. The Quinteros got here early. Now they're late."

It wasn't much of a town, just the single broad street running parallel with the bank of the Rio Grande for three hundred yards. Halfway down the narrow strip of Tamaulipas state between Nuevo Leon and Texas. Twin rows of single story adobe buildings with the stockyards blocking off one end. A town with an insecure toehold in the cattle business trying unsuccessfully to compete with the Texas towns of Laredo and Brownsville as a holding depot for the cross-border beef trade.

The signs of its lack of success were plain to see in the neglect of many of the buildings and the complete abandonment of others. With the exception of the tiny *Federale* post, all the buildings were business premises, established to fill the needs of transient Mexican *vaqueros* and American cowpunchers.

As he led his heat-weary horse diagonally across the street and hitched the reins to a post outside an open

27

dry goods store, Edge was aware of the aura of depression that pervaded the town in the early afternoon. He had sensed this when he first rode in from the west in the cool early morning. And perhaps this was why he had elected to spend some time here—and the last of his money on feed and stabling for his horse and a meager breakfast for himself—rather than to cross the Rio Grande shallows into Texas.

For, as the young son of the cantina owner had noted, the half-breed was himself despondent behind his outer shell of impassiveness. It gave him an affinity with a town suffering the bitter effects of unfulfilled hopes.

Now he sensed a deeper and blacker mood of failure permeating through the oppressive heat that draped the town. And mixed in with this a menacing enmity. A dangerous combination of emotions that came together in the expressions on the faces of the Mexican man and his wife behind the counter in the under-stocked dry goods store. The couple were old and stoop-shouldered, unafraid of whatever else a long and hard life might choose to torment them with.

"How does it feel, *señor?*" the man asked in a croaking voice. "To kill a whole town with two bullets? The brothers Quintero and their cattle were our last hope."

While the *Federale* sergeant was learning the facts of the shooting, many faces had appeared briefly at the cantina windows. They had seen and heard enough to broadcast the basic details of the incident.

"Be obliged if you'd get me six cartons of forty-five caliber shells," Edge answered, and turned his attention to a meager display of headgear.

"Gringo bastards!" the old woman hissed through compressed lips as the half-breed took off his ill-used sombrero and tried on a low-crowned, wide-brimmed black Stetson.

He placed the sombrero on the stand where the Stetson had been and returned to the counter. "How much for the hat and the shells, *señora?*" he asked evenly as the old man came painfully erect from crouching at a low shelf.

His bristled face was set in an easy expression, but the glinting, ice-like blueness of his slitted eyes overruled every other feature.

The old woman remained unafraid, holding his gaze and responding to it with growing hatred in her own eyes. "We do not do business with murderers!" she hissed, and went to sweep the cartons of bullets off the counter top.

But Edge caught hold of her wrist as her arm started its swing. She vented a grunt of surprised anger and her husband uttered a low cry of alarm. Edge leaned forward and lowered himself so that he could scoop up the cartons in the crook of his free arm and press them to his side.

"I always pay my way, *señora.* How much?"

"Five dollars to be rid of you!" the anxious old man replied quickly.

The half-breed nodded, released the thin wrist and delved into his hip pocket. He produced his roll, peeled off a five-dollar bill and dropped it on the counter. As he turned to go toward the door, the incensed woman snatched up the five spot and tore into shreds in hands that looked suddenly like claws. Then she spat on the pieces before scattering them to the floor.

"That is what I think of your blood money, murderer!" she shrieked, her dark eyes blazing.

"Easy come, easy go," Edge replied from the doorway, and raked his own cold-eyed gaze over the dusty stock of the store. "But I figure you worked hard to build up this place."

"*Si!*" the man muttered sorrowfully. "And it was for nothing now that the Quinteros are dead."

"Hard got, hard to lose," the half-breed said, striking a match on the doorframe and dropping it on a tinder-dry pile of shirts. Horror became instantly inscribed upon the wrinkled faces of the elderly couple. But Edge spoke again before they could give voice to their feelings. "Gringo I'll let go, *señor*. But my ma and pa were married a full two years before I was born. So I get real fired up when somebody calls me a bastard."

"Agua!" the woman shrieked, and shoved her husband toward a doorway in back of the counter.

Flames leapt up from the pile of shirts, then tongued to the side, and began to rage on bolts of cloth and a display of pants when Edge swung a boot into the seat of the blaze.

"May you suffer the agonies of eternal damnation!" the woman berated, and was gripped by a bout of choked coughing as black smoke filled the store.

"I'm in training for it," Edge answered and pulled open the door. *"Hasta la vista, señora."*

As he closed the door, the old man hurled a pail of water toward the fire. It fell short, only a few droplets splashing to hissing extinction in the flames.

As Edge mounted the gelding, leaned forward to unhitch the reins and eased his mount into a walk. His sense of being watched by hostile eyes was very strong. Not from the dry goods store with smoke wisping out of the cracks between door and frame, for the old couple were too heavily engaged in fighting the effects of arousing his cold rage. But from every other occupied building on either side of the sun-bright street, hate emanated with almost a palpable pressure.

The hate was not directed exclusively at the slow-riding half-breed, though. For the town had loathing to spare, and shared some of it with the group of *vaqueros* and three Americans who waited at the Rio Grande ford across from the stockyard.

Edge was unperturbed by the depth of feeling generated toward him. He was simply concerned to remain alert should malice spur violent reaction. Thus, although he appeared nonchalantly at ease as he rode, he was actually tense and poised to respond to the first hint of danger.

The War Between the States had taught him how to keep constant watch without strain, along with a thousand other lessons in the art of survival as he rode with the US Cavalry, first as a lieutenant and then a captain. Facing as much danger from certain of the troopers under his command as from the gray-clad enemy.

Josiah C. Hedges was not unique in being dehumanized by the brutalities of war. And, like the vast majority who survived without serious physical harm, he rode home after Appomattox with a firm resolve to preserve within himself only the good of what he had been as a youth and grown into as a man.

But it was not meant to be.

For the six Union troopers, who had come close to killing him often during the war, reached the Iowa farm ahead of him. And left one of their number dead alongside the horribly tortured corpse of Jamie in the scorched garden of the burnt-out house.

In tracking down and extracting terrible vengeance on the killers of his brother, the newly discharged soldier called upon every hard-learned lesson in evil and viciousness that the war had taught him to destroy everything that stood in his path. Including human life. And when another ex-soldier named Elliot Thombs spilled his life blood on the earth of Kansas, Josiah C. Hedges was wanted for murder. And took the new name of Edge.

"You should know, *señora*," the sweating *Federale* sergeant said as Edge rode past the wagon onto which he was helping the undertaker load the now occupied

31

coffins. "The Quintero brothers each leave a widow and three orphan children."

The half-breed reined his horse to a halt and nodded toward the quiet cattle in the stockyards. "That the Quinteros' herd?"

"*Si.* Worth much money. But money cannot buy back life for the dead."

"But it pays for burying them, feller," Edge countered flatly as he heeled his horse forward to continue his slow progress along the street.

The *Federale* stared after the departing figure with depthless scorn in his gaze.

"*Sargento!*" the owner of the dry goods store yelled, emerging from his doorway in a cloud of billowing smoke. "The *gringo* has set fire to my place! Help! Get help for us!"

Edge halted his horse again and swung his head around to look back at the *Federale*. He was in time to see him give one of the coffins a final shove to set it firmly on the undertaker's wagon. Then whirl and reach for his holstered revolver.

"The old woman played with fire when she insulted my parents, feller," the half-breed said coldly. "You touch that gun and it won't be just your fingers get burned."

The man allowed his rage to cool and dropped his gun hand to his side. "One day you will suffer greatly for what you are, *señor!*" he rasped, then turned and started to run toward the burning store.

"Who do you mean, one day?" Edge asked quietly, so that only he heard the words as he faced front again and ordered the gelding into movement.

Behind him, people emerged from buildings to converge on the scene of the fire, some of them carrying slopping pails.

"That was a real lousy thing to do, Edge!" Ezekiel

32

Taggart accused, swinging clumsily up into the saddle of a powerful looking white stallion.

"Yeah, real lousy," the half-breed agreed. "Maybe that's why I had the itch to do it."

The others swung astride their horses, the elder Taggart as awkward as his son.

"Man, I'm glad you're on our side," Barney Tait growled as heat shattered the display window of the store and flames spurted out, driving back the fire-fighters.

"Won't make no difference if you ever call me a bastard again, feller."

Tait swallowed hard, recalling his use of the word after Edge had removed the threat of the razor. "Hell, it's just a figure of speech," he complained as the half-breed took the lead in easing his horse into the shallow water.

"Maybe that's all it amounts to," came the reply as more horses splashed reluctantly into the broad, muddy Rio Grande. "But it just got a store totalled."

Chapter Four

THE sun-glinting spray kicked up by the pumping hooves of the horses provided a slight and fleeting relief from the harsh heat of the day as the riders crossed the river. Its cooling dampness bathed their sweat-sheened faces and soaked through their clothing to dilute the tacky perspiration that pasted the coarse fabric to the flesh of their bodies and limbs.

But then they rode up onto the Texas bank of the Rio Grande and the sun that beat down was as brutally hot as it had been in Mexico, and the dust was as fine and as clinging. So that, within minutes of entering the United States, the men's clothes and exposed flesh were again soaked with sticky sweat, which tenaciously held onto the dust erupted by the slow moving animals. The horses, too, became as uniformly gray as the men astride them.

"You been back there long?" Barney Tait asked, licking salt-tasting dust off his lips and spitting the saliva between the ears of his black stallion.

"Since this morning," Edge answered.

They were riding beside each other at the head of the group. The Taggart father and son were behind them and the *vaqueros* were strung out in pairs and singly. The last place in the line was taken by the doleful-eyed old-timer who seemed unconcerned that this position meant he was eating the dust of everyone else in the group.

"There was a lot of talk about the Quinteros?" the Big-T foreman probed.

The half-breed pursed his lips. "How much of my life story do you want to hear, feller?"

Tait scowled.

"Edge isn't the kind of man who appreciates those tactics, Barney," old man Taggart growled. "And neither are you. So best you ask him direct, I think."

Edge showed a bleak grin as he waited for Tait to think of a new opening. And he continued to maintain an easy surveillance on the south Texas terrain they were traveling. It was a parched landscape of low hills flanking broad valleys, sparsely scattered with patches of tough grass and clumps of brush with, here and there, an occasional stunted tree—mesquite, juniper and scrub oak. But most of the vegetation was cactus, growing more strongly than anything else because it required less from the arid ground to sustain it. These living things provided shapes without contrasting colors for, like the men and horses who moved among them, they were cloaked with the fine, gray dust of the parched earth in which they grew. So there was just the yellow fire of the sun against the solid bright blueness of the sky to add a vivid counterpoint to the monotonous tones of the neutral ground beneath.

The younger Taggart had less patience than the half-breed. "We want to know if those Mexican cattlemen had anything to do with Matt Saxby," he blurted. "Or if they were upset simply because we took their outfit away from them."

Tait spat again, irritated at the Easterners for horning into the exchange. "Yeah. You said you'd heard about them guys being good with guns."

"From a couple of their line riders," Edge supplied. "Had breakfast with them on the Quintero spread south of Lampazos about a week ago. Never have heard of anyone called Matt Saxby."

35

"Was top hand of the Big-T," Tait said quickly, as if anxious to block further interruptions from the Taggarts. "But he ain't no more. Word is he's out roundin' up men instead of cows. Kind of men who'll . . ."

He turned to look at the bristled, sweat-run, dusty profile of Edge, interrupting his flow.

"But you got to me before he did," the half-breed said evenly into the pause.

Tait was again disconcerted, not trusting Edge's apparent indifference. "I didn't mean . . ."

"I am what I am, feller. And I ain't either proud or ashamed of it . . ." He paused himself now, before he added, "Any more."

There had been times in the life of the man called Edge when he had experienced the basic human emotions of shame and pride. But that had been far back in the long period of years between two deaths—the finding of the buzzard-ravaged corpse of Jamie on the Iowa farmstead and turning to see the lifeless form of Isabella Montez sprawled in the dust of a Mexican village called San Parral.

And he had felt other normal human responses, too. Perhaps every one from love to hate. All this in a time after the war in which he thought he had been drained of the capacity to experience any depth of feeling that was not rooted in evil. So he had suffered more from mental anguish than physical pain as he followed the endless violent trail that zig-zagged over half a continent between the farmstead and the village. Always leaving and hardly ever arriving. Fighting a lone war against an enemy far more powerful than the entire Confederate forces had been—his own destiny that had ordained, as he had told the old woman in the dry goods store, that his life should be nothing more than a training session for the purgatory he would suffer after death.

On occasions he had been tricked into believing he

had achieved victory. Most vivid in his memory was the marriage to Elizabeth Day and their brief period of happiness on another farmstead, this time in the Dakotas. But Beth died more terribly than Jamie and, because he was still able to respond normally, Edge had endured grief.

But he had spilled no tears for Isabella, who he thought he had loved as deeply as Beth and who he would certainly have married had she not been gunned down in San Parral.

And so he knew, as he rode out of the village watched by a young boy the same age as the son of the cantina owner in the cow town on the Rio Grande, that he had won something over his fate. He was at last totally without emotion, indifferently callous to the results of the evil and violence that were always close to wherever he happened to be. Thus, he would never again have to suffer the harsh agonies of a mind tormented by such futile emotions as grief, remorse or the thirst for vengeance. Because such responses had to be triggered by others—from mere desire to a need to love. And the death of Isabella and his reaction to it had proved he was equally immune to these.

Yet the boy in the cantina had detected a degree of sadness beneath the surface of the man. That was an emotion.

"You're too jumpy, Tait!" Ezekiel Taggart accused. "Those Mexicans were ranchers. And rich ones, I'd say. They wouldn't hire themselves out to Saxby for a few dollars."

"You asked him, too!" Tait snapped.

"Calm down, both of you!" the elder Taggart growled. "Edge here has made sure we don't have to worry about those Quinteros any more. But if it makes any difference, I agree with Zeke. They were just mad because we outbid them for the men. I'd have felt the

37

same if somebody bought my outfit out from under my nose."

"How did you lose them, feller?" the half-breed asked, not having to rely on Tait to lead the way to the Big-T spread. For the sign left by the Taggarts and their foreman on the ride south was still plain to see in the dust.

Tait was taking a drink from one of his canteens. He swilled the tepid water around in his mouth and decided to swallow it instead of spitting it over the head of his horse. "The bastards quit on me!" he snarled. "They rounded up the friggin' critters like everythin' was fine and they didn't have no gripes. Then the sons-ofbitches just up and rode off the spread. Leavin' me with five thousand head of trail-ready cows and no one to help drive them!"

Edge glanced over his shoulder at the grim-faced Taggart and his irritable son. "Which one of you is going to tell it straight this time?" he asked.

"All right, all right!" Tait growled. "The Big-T ain't the best spread in Texas to work on. We pay low and we expect every man in the outfit to work his butt off every minute he ain't in the sack. We can do that because there's more cowpunchers than there are jobs for them. Most times, the hired hands just complain or beat it. If they beat it, there's always been others to take their places. The new ones soon get to gripin' the same as the rest." He managed a brief, cynical smile. "It's dealin' with all the friggin' complaints that got me the bad mouth I'm known for."

He opened his mouth wide as if he was about to demonstrate his ability to bawl out miscreant cowhands. But instead he tossed a plug of tobacco against the back of his throat and began to chew some juice out of it.

"But then that shit-stirrer Saxby showed up," he continued, and abruptly there was venom in his tone.

38

"I guess I should have spotted there was somethin' wrong about the bastard when he didn't do no gripin'. Just did his work real well and never put up no arguments about the hours and the pay. I even promoted him top hand, on account of how he knew cowpunchin' so well."

"Zeke and I live in New York," Taggart supplied without invitation. "I left the Big-T completely in Barney's hands as far as the day-to-day running of the place was concerned."

"You just made the rules, uh?" Edge asked.

"I own it!" came the irate reply. "And I require the highest return on every investment I make."

"I ain't complaining, feller," the half-breed said evenly. "Just sorry I never got into the cattle business before if the rates you pay are so low."

"You know better than that, Edge!" Tait rasped. He jerked a thumb over his shoulder to indicate the strangely quiet *vaqueros* strung out behind the Taggarts. "What them and you are bein' paid is a small fortune compared to even the top rates for trail drivin'. But we been backed into a corner by the law of supply and demand."

"Ain't no corners out on the open trail with five thousand head of cattle," Edge countered. "Which makes it rough when the shooting starts."

"Okay, okay!" This time the stream of saliva that was directed between the ears of the stallion was stained brown by tobacco juice. "That, too. Mr. Taggart and me didn't want no hagglin'. If you'd stayed in the cantina, you'd have heard what I told these Mexicans. We need 'em bad, so we know we gotta pay high. But there weren't no sense in leavin' it rest there. So I told them the pay's extra high on account of the risk from that sonofabitch Saxby."

"He can afford to hire guns on what the Big-T paid him, feller?"

39

"I dunno if the rumor's true or not," Tait growled. "Just tellin' you what I do know. Day Mr. Oscar Taggart and his son showed up at the spread, Saxby called a meetin' of the whole outfit. Said that if we didn't pay 'em extra back pay and up our rates for the drive, they'd walk out on us. And see to it that no man within fifty miles of Laredo would work for the Big-T."

"And we called them!" Oscar Taggart rasped. "Then fooled them when they pulled out. Came across the border for Mexican labor."

"Whose taking care of the herd right now?" Edge asked.

"Four deputies outta Laredo," the tobacco chewing foreman answered. "It was one of them said he'd heard Saxby was hirin' pro gunslingers."

"Personally, I doubt it," old man Taggart said thoughtfully. "Even if he could raise the money, it wouldn't look good for them high ideals he talks about having."

"So why did you hire Edge?" the tobacco-chewing foreman asked pointedly.

"Let me finish, man!" Taggart snapped. "I don't reckon he's got any more ideals than you, me or anybody else in the cattle raising business. He's just out to make a name for himself. But not the kind you get setting professional gunmen on honest people going about their lawful business."

"Same question, Mr. Taggart," Tait insisted. He had been watching the half-breed surreptitiously and taken note of the way the glinting slits of his eyes constantly raked the sun-baked terrain. And this relentless watchfulness started to unnerve the foreman. His anxiety could be heard in the tone of his voice, and seen in his own, much more obvious vigil.

"I told you to let me finish!" his boss snarled. "Saxby's making himself out to be some kind of messiah, sent specially to get a better deal for cowhands. So he's not about to lay himself open to trouble from the law and all the bad publicity that would get him. But he's a hot-head deep down inside. And it's a long way from the spread to Laramie. The farther north we get, the more it will rile him. Because he's committed to making the Big-T his test. So there's no telling what he'll do to stop us if he thinks we're going to make it to the end of the trail. That, Barney, is why I hired Mr. Edge."

"You're actin' like you don't go along with that line of thinkin'," Tait muttered to the half-breed.

"Why's that, feller?"

"Way you're watchin' like you expect to see trouble behind every rock."

"Like chewing tobacco."

"Uh?"

"Habit."

"One that impresses me," Oscar Taggart said grimly.

"It gives me the friggin' heebie-jeebies," the stocky foreman murmured.

"Relax, feller," Edge said evenly. "I'll let you know when to be scared."

Tait spat the whole wad of chewed out tobacco over the head of his horse now. "Thanks for nothin'!" he growled sourly.

"A hundred and fifty dollars a week is not nothing, Tait," Zeke Taggart pointed out, and sounded almost as embittered as the man riding ahead of him.

"No sweat," Edge told Tait.

"Maybe not for you, mister. But I feel like I'm friggin' meltin'. And it ain't just because of that stinkin' sun up there!"

Behind the four Americans the *vaqueros* remained silent, as nervous as Barney Tait. But their mood owed nothing to Edge's present attitude, for they had shown signs of their misgivings from the moment they gathered on the south bank of the Rio Grande.

41

Perhaps then it had simply been that they regretted the killing of their previous employers and, like the townspeople, had begun to consider the implications of what had happened. In the fetid atmosphere and relative comfort of the cantina, their hip pockets bulged by American dollars, they had been concerned only with the moment. Except for the old-timer. But outside, in the bright, harsh, blistering sunlight they faced reality and experienced the first pangs of doubt.

And as they were led deeper into Texas, doubt grew toward fear, the money in their pockets becoming less and less important to them.

Edge did not care enough about the Mexicans to consciously consider what was running through their minds as they sat on their slow-moving horses. But he had sufficient experience in dealing with men to be aware of why this group was so morosely taciturn. They were cattlemen, tough and hard because of the nature of their work. But just ordinary men—some with homes and families, maybe—prey to the weakness of greed. Dazzled by Taggart money to buy luxuries for themselves or necessities for their dependants.

But out here in the hostile wilderness of south Texas—with the prospect of the long trail to Laramie—money was so much excess baggage. Even though he was in a crowd, each man was somehow alone. With time to examine his motives and reflect on his mistakes. Each of the dejected *vaqueros* must surely have been pondering the risks that Barney Tait had warned him about. And comparing the new job with the old. The old had been hard and low paid. But the work was regular and free of dangers, if a man knew his trade. In the new job, only one member of the Big-T outfit had the specialist skills the foreman had predicted would be needed.

"There they are, the beautiful critters!" Tait exclaimed gleefully—almost lovingly.

The Texan's mood had lightened as soon as they rode through an arched gap in a wire fence—passing under a sign proclaiming: TAGGART BIG-T—PRIVATE PROPERTY—KEEP OUT. Beyond the fence the landscape continued to be an undulating panorama of gentle hills. But the grass grew in more extensive patchs and there were stands of timber instead of individual trees. Further into the Taggart spread, wind-driven water pumps provided an additional feature to the landscape. The grass and foliage was greener. Cowpats were everywhere, dried and brittle beneath the hooves of the horses. Occasionally the group rode past the bleached skeleton of an animal, which had died and been left to the scavengers.

It was good cattle raising country, well supplied with water from underground springs, and not over-grazed. And it was obvious to the ever-watchful Edge that Barney Tait—only foreman of the spread—had a great sense of pride in the Big-T. While the owner and his son felt nothing for it, except for a mild relief that they no longer had to endure the irritation of rising dust clinging to their sun-reddened, sweat-oozing faces.

Tait gave voice to his new-found happiness as he and the half-breed led the others out from a fold between two curving hills and saw the vast herd of longhorn cattle. It was below them, the closest steers over a mile away, at the lowest point in a huge natural crater encircled by verdant hills. On the western slope was the ranch house, a frame building constructed to two stories at the front and one at the rear to take account of the incline. The house, four forage-store barns and a stable and bunkhouse block were fenced off and from a distance the whole place looked neat and well cared for.

The cattle also looked in prime condition as they grazed contentedly on a square mile of pasture, unperturbed by the restrictive barbed wire, stranded between posts, which had been erected just for the round-up.

Five men were standing guard on the herd—one more than Tait had said there was. Four of them patrolled the perimeter fence astride horses while the fifth stood beside his mount in the shade of a large oak growing in a corner of the ranch house yard.

"Thank God they're still where we left them," Zeke Taggart rasped.

"I told you, son," his father reminded acidly. "Saxby wouldn't dare start that kind of trouble with the Laredo sheriff's office taking care of our interests."

"Who's the extra man, feller?" Edge asked.

It was obvious that the group of men angling across the south western curve of the basin had been seen by all the guards. But no hand was raised in greeting. Those on horseback continued to patrol the barbed wire fence while the one beneath the tree watched the approach of the riders crossing the slope.

"Sheriff O'Brian," Tait supplied, and seemed to have difficulty in tearing his attention away from the quiet cattle. "Not a bad guy, for a lawman."

"From my dealings with him, he's a good man as long as you stay on the right side of him, Edge," Oscar Taggart added, his tone cautionary.

"Which side is that, feller?" the half-breed asked, as the Laredo sheriff raised an arm in a signal and then wearily mounted his horse.

"The inside of the law," Tait answered absently on behalf of his boss. For the closer he rode to the herd the less attention he paid to anything else.

"Something you know very little about, I'd say," Zeke Taggart growled sullenly, as the four deputies responded to the sheriff's sign, heeling their horses into a canter to close on him as he rode out from under the shade of the oak.

"Quit needling, Ezekiel!" Taggart scolded his son grimly.

44

Edge looked back over his shoulder to show the slits of his glinting eyes to the younger Taggart. "Always figure laws to be like men, feller," he said evenly. "Some you just have to respect. Others are made to be broken."

Zeke grimaced, electing not to hold the half-breed's level gaze. Instead, he transferred his distaste to the quiet cattle, wrinkling his nostrils at the stink of them.

"I'll check 'em out, Mr. Taggart," Tait said.

"And post guards," the owner of the herd snapped. "My son will take his turn."

Zeke seemed about to protest, but was held in sullen silence by his father's angry scowl. Tait snapped his fingers and pointed at three of the *vaqueros*. The Mexicans veered away from the column in the wake of the Big-T foreman, less tense now that they had to deal with a job they knew instead of having to combat fears of the unknown. Zeke followed them with glowering ill-humor as his father moved his horse up alongside Edge's gelding.

"I'd ask you not to take too much notice of Ezekiel, Mr. Edge. He was born and bred in the city and has been rather insulated from the harsher sides of life by my wealth. His mother spoiled him and I . . ." He broke off as he realized the half-breed was not interested in what he was saying. He gazed after his son with forlorn sadness in his dull green eyes. "Well, I worry about him," he concluded morosely.

Edge merely glanced toward the younger Taggart, growing smaller as he reached the foot of the slope to take up a position on the fence indicated by Tait. "I'd say you got nothing much to worry about," he murmured, then spat dusty saliva to the side. "On account that nothing much bothers me."

45

Chapter Five

OSCAR TAGGART briefly showed his anger. Then he sighed.

"I've a fond hope that bringing him out West will make something of him," he said quietly, then pushed the problem of his son to the back of his mind. He raised a hand and his voice. "Good afternoon, Sheriff! There's been no trouble?"

The Laredo lawman was in his early fifties. Short and thick-set, running to fat about his middle. His sun-darkened face was fleshy with features that, in repose, suggested a mind concerned only with the distasteful things of life. He responded to the greeting with a slight nod, then ignored Taggart for several moments as he surveyed Edge and the Mexicans. When he had made his appraisal, completing it as the body of riders halted horses a few feet in front of him and his deputies, his expression remained pointedly displeased. The four younger men aligned behind him were relieved that their cow guarding duty was finished, and impatient to leave the Big-T range.

"Ain't been none around here," O'Brian drawled.

The owner of the Big-T started a smile, but interrupted it to concentrate on awkwardly dismounting from his horse. The expression showed signs of strain as he stood on the ground and squinted up at the lawman. "I was just passing the time of day," he said.

"You said Saxby wouldn't move against me while we're in your jurisdiction and I had faith in that."

"But trouble's brewin' in town," the sheriff went on as if there had been no intervention from Taggart. "Word of what you hired in Mexico came ahead of you and ain't no one raised a cheer about it, that's for sure."

"So they ain't come to welcome us then?" Edge asked wryly, nodding up toward the rim of the basin above the ranch house.

All attention switched hurriedly away from the soft-spoken half-breed toward the point on the high ground he had indicated. What they saw was a group of perhaps twenty horsemen, riding close together at a canter, making dust on a wheel-rutted trail that curved down the slope to finish in front of the ranch house where the watchers were waiting.

Taggart's smile was transformed into an anxious grimace, until O'Brian drawled, "I'll handle it."

He shifted his gaze away from Taggart to linger on the impassive face of Edge, and he altered his expression to give the words he spoke more force. "Two men dead in one day better be enough for you, mister."

"More than enough, feller," the half-breed replied evenly. "But sometimes it works out I can't live without killing . . ."

"You're off duty, Edge!" Taggart cut in. "The sheriff is charged with our protection in this county."

The smile was completely gone from Taggart's ruddy face now, and the sounds of cantering hooves beat through the hot, cow-tainted air of the Texas afternoon.

"If you're happy, I'm happy," Edge allowed easily as the *vaqueros* toyed nervously with their reins.

O'Brian and his deputies wheeled their horses to form a defensive line across the end of the trail, facing the group of riders who slowed their advance as they made

47

a final turn around a large barn at the corner of the yard. Then the larger group came to a halt in response to a hand signal from a man who had always been a few feet out in front of the rest.

They were aged between twenty and forty; hard looking men with work-roughened hands and complexions stained by climatic extremes. They were molded in all shapes and sizes but each appeared to possess an equal share of physical strength, whatever his individual build. They were dressed in workaday cowhand garb with few frills or affectations. Each wore a gunbelt with a revolver in the holster. Most included a booted rifle among the accouterments slung from their saddles.

"You ain't come out here to listen to me read the riot act again, Saxby," the sheriff drawled.

The man at the head of the newly arrived group was about thirty. He was lean, six feet tall, with a lazy, loose-limbed way of sitting his horse. His face was classically handsome, his good looks enhanced by blond hair which poked untidily out from under the brim of his hat and yet was neatly trimmed in long sideburns. There was a grim intensity in his brown eyes and a broad hint of hard-to-shake resolution in the thrust of his jaw.

"I came to talk to the Big-T's new outfit, Sheriff," Matt Saxby answered. There was a drawl in his voice, but his origins were further east than Texas.

O'Brian's head swung from side to side, showing his displeasure to all the men behind Saxby. "Seems you got somethin' real interestin' to say. Seein' as how those boys rode all the way out from Laredo to hear it."

"They didn't come here to start anything, Sheriff. But I'm no hero. Especially when I'm up against some high-priced, sharp-shooting pro gunman."

He moved his intense gaze toward Edge, who nodded

48

and smiled a wry greeting. "North of the border it seems I come cheaper, feller."

Saxby furrowed his brow as Edge swung down from the saddle. "How's that, mister?"

There was an open five-bar gate in the fence around the yard and the half-breed led his gelding through it. "Seems one of the customs hereabouts is for the law to handle differences of opinion. Makes me duty free."

"Speak your piece!" O'Brian barked at Saxby as Edge hitched the gelding's reins to a low hanging bow of the oak and then squatted on an exposed root in the dappled shade of the foliage. "And make it fast. Me and my boys are sick of smellin' cows."

Saxby jerked a thumb toward the herd grazing quietly inside the fence at the base of the big hollow below the ranch house. "Them men down there oughta hear it as well."

The three *vaqueros* and Zeke Taggart, who rode slowly around the perimeter fence, were paying scant attention to the cattle they were assigned to watch. Instead, they tilted back their heads to gaze anxiously up the grassy slope. While Barney Tait appeared to be unaware of the existence of any living thing apart from himself and a steer he was examining at the far side of the herd.

"Reckon you're not the only man who likes to hear the sound of his own voice, mister," the sheriff drawled. "They get to hear what you have to say."

Saxby was ready to press his objection, but the strength of determination visible on O'Brian's fleshy face warned him it would be a waste of time. So the good-looking, blond cowhand stood up in his stirrups to look over the heads of the quartet of deputies and the sheriff, and stare intently at the nervous Mexicans behind them.

"Listen, you men. Listen well, so you can tell your buddies about this. You don't know what you're getting into, working for the Big-T outfit." He waved an arm to indicate the grim-faced men on their horses behind him. "These boys know what it was like before. I know that, too. We've all worked for the Big-T. For that slave-driving Tait, throwing his weight around on behalf of the rich living owner of the spread. Low pay and long hours are nothing new to men in our business. But the Big-T's always paid its hands the lowest and wanted the most out of them. We aim to change that . . ."

"And you have, Saxby!" Oscar Taggart cut in harshly. Then grinned as he half turned to sweep an arm toward the nervously confused *vaqueros*. "These men are being paid better than any hands that ever herded cattle before."

Saxby's brown eyes expressed blatant contempt. "For two reasons, Taggart! If you ever do play them more than the come-on money! You knew you had to pay high to get hands, out of necessity! And out of spite you took your big money offer across the border!"

"Ranching's a business, mister!" Taggart snarled, provoked by the other man's low-voiced bitterness. "And when someone does all he can to ruin a business, the owner has to . . ."

The handsome blond standing in his stirrups was abruptly infected by the older man's fury, and his tone became as harsh as Taggart's as he interrupted.

"I'm through trading words with the Big-T bosses!" he flung at the man on the ground, and then ignored him to direct his words at the Mexicans. "All right, you men have got a hundred dollars each in your pockets! And maybe when you get to Laramie the Big-T will pay you the rest of what's promised! You'll need every lousy cent of it, because you won't ever work again in the cattle business! On either side of the Rio Grande!"

50

Taggart snorted and suddenly stooped to grab a handful of dust. "You're built big, mister!" he snapped, and opened his hand so that the dust motes could float back down to the ground. "But in the cattle business you're smaller than one grain of that!"

Saxby nodded, but still refused to look at the man. "Twenty hands rode out here with me," he told the *vaqueros,* moderating his tone. "But every ranch and trail hand between Laredo and Brownsville is with us in spirit. And the word about the Big-T is being spread west to El Paso and north to the railheads in Kansas, Colorado, Nebraska and Wyoming. No man will work with you in an American outfit if you lift a finger to move the Big-T herd. And no man will touch a single cow that comes across the border if he knows you men helped raise or drive it. But that don't have to happen. Not if you pay back right now the money you've been given and ride off the Big-T spread."

The doubts that the Mexicans had experienced during the long ride from the river crossing were now broadened and deepened. They considered their anxieties in isolation, or traded perplexed frowns with each other.

Saxby and the American cowhands saw this and began to smile. Oscar Taggart's rage built as he sensed imminent defeat. The five lawmen remained neutrally grim-faced between the two factions. Edge, smoking a cigarette in the pleasant shade of the oak tree, continued to look at the ravages of neglect and decay that had taken their toll of the expensively built ranch house and out-buildings. When he had first seen the place from a distance it had been shrouded by heat haze. In close up, the bright sunlight emphasized the signs of dilapidation.

"You men signed contracts!" Taggart raged.

"But, *señor,*" a Mexican with two front teeth missing countered. "We did not realize what we were . . ."

51

"You were told you were not getting paid a fortune for a routine cattle drive!" Taggart snarled.

Saxby had reseated himself in his saddle. Now he rose erect in his stirrups again. "Without you *vaqueros,* the Big-T is finished! A contract with an outfit that doesn't exist is no contract at all!"

The Mexicans considered this, then nodded. Some even showed faint smiles of relief—honest, law-abiding men out of their depth, grateful to be tossed a lifeline.

And there was a trace of desperation on Taggart's sun-reddened face as he swung his enraged eyes between the complacent Saxby and the eager Mexicans. And in his voice as he snapped, "Edge!"

The half-breed curtailed his indifferent survey of the house, with its cracked window panes and peeling paintwork, and the out-buildings, with their carelessly patched shingles and leaning doors. He interrupted the time-killing comparisons he had been making between the neglected state of the buildings and the fine condition of the steers.

"Sheriff's the legal expert, feller," he said. "But the way I see it, the contract's good as long as you've got the money to back it."

Now Taggart nodded, with greater enthusiasm than the Mexicans. "That's damn right!" He flung out an arm to point at the herd below. "And you've only to look down there to see there's money enough to back the contract a hundred times over!"

O'Brian snorted. "You all through talkin', mister?" he asked Saxby.

"No, I'm not! Not until I'm sure these men are absolutely certain of where they stand. I want to repeat . . ."

"If all you got to say is what you've already said, you're all through," the lawman drawled. "So turn your horses around and ride outta here."

His glowering eyes shifted to the left and the right to

insure that all the men behind Saxby saw his determination to end the confrontation. When he fixed his gaze back on Saxby's face he was met with a stare of equal resolution.

"Sure, Sheriff," Saxby allowed. "We'll turn around and ride off this lousy spread. Just as soon as the Mexicans do."

O'Brian sighed wearily and turned his head to look at the *vaqueros*. "You boys hear him. You gonna leave?"

The dark-skinned faces in the shade of broad-brimmed sombreros expressed dismay that although the line they had been thrown was still there, they had to make some effort to use it as a way out of their dilemma. Then the man with two teeth missing nodded. And eyed Taggart miserably.

"We are sorry, *señor*. We made a mistake. There was much drinking in the cantina before you came."

"Edge!" Taggart snarled as the rest of the Mexicans acknowledged their agreement with what one of their number had said. "Shoot the first Big-T hand that makes a move to leave."

The half-breed became the center of fearful and angry attention as he rose from the tree root and slid the Winchester rifle from its boot.

"No, feller," he replied as he canted the rifle to his shoulder and the sheriff and deputies draped hands over their holstered Colts.

"You'll do what you're told, damnit!" Taggart blustered.

"What I am doing," Edge countered in the same easy tone as before, moving up to the warped and leaning yard fence and resting the Winchester barrel across the top bar—aimed at the sky above Saxby's head. "My job is to see your herd gets to Laramie. And dead men ride no trails."

"So what's with the rifle?" Saxby growled, unafraid.

53

Edge pumped the lever action to jack a shell into the breech. O'Brian snorted as he and his deputies drew their revolvers half out of the holsters. Several of the men behind Saxby gripped the butts of holstered handguns or reached for the stocks of rifles jutting from boots. But the half-breed's Winchester remained angled toward the harsh blueness of the sky and nobody drew a weapon against him.

"On a point of principle, it'll kill the first man who aims a gun at me," the tall, lean, dark-skinned man at the fence replied. "On a point of law, it'll kill up to a dozen trespassers on Big-T property. More if I get the time to reload."

"I warned you, mister!" O'Brian snarled.

"And Edge has warned you, Sheriff!" Taggart countered. "You have my thanks for taking care of things while Tait and my son and I were engaged elsewhere. But that job's over. We're back now. And well able to handle the Big-T without the help of the law."

The half-breed's reaction to Taggart's backing was just a slight parting of his lips to show the merest hint of a smile.

"In a pig's eye!" O'Brian roared. "You can't just hire and fire the law, mister!"

"On your way, feller," Edge said evenly. "You're a peace officer. Keep the peace by setting an example to this savior of the downtrodden and his converts."

The smile was gone now, replaced by glinting-eyed contempt for the shocked and confused cowhands.

"Matt!" a man with a knife scar on his right cheek growled. "There's just Taggart and the gunslinger. And Taggart ain't even armed. The greasers we can forget."

Three other men in the group from Laredo nodded their approval of the uneven odds. Saxby was not among them.

"I told you men!" he snapped. "I came out here to talk is all. No trouble."

54

He wheeled his horse to face the cowhands. Not until they all showed their willingness to comply with his leadership—the scar-faced men and three others reluctantly—did he turn his intense gaze on the Mexicans. "You people have been told the facts. Up to what you do now."

Then he faced front again and the group of hands jostled their horses to open up a passage for him to ride through.

A relieved looking O'Brian signaled for his deputies to close in on the group. But held back himself to glare malevolently down at the tense and sweating face of Oscar Taggart.

"You been lucky, mister," he rasped between tightly clenched teeth. "Because I take my job seriously enough to believe that the law's for the protection of every citizen who ain't breakin' it. But there ain't many peace officers like me. So I figure that outside of my county, you—and the help your money can buy and the people your hired gun can scare—are on your own. And if I was a religious man, I'd pray you get what you deserve."

"Thank you for your good wishes, Sheriff," Taggart replied, confident of his victory in this encounter. "Since it's my experience that if a man wants to succeed badly enough, then he will. I therefore deserve to get my beef to the Laramie stockyards."

O'Brian's rage expanded as he searched his mind for a retort. Then had his attention wrenched away from the smiling Taggart by the sharp crack of a rifle shot. And the choked cry of a man in pain.

He, and everyone else, looked from the smoking muzzle of the half-breed's Winchester to the scar-faced man. He was half turned in his saddle, his left hand clenched around the wrist of his right. His right hand was folded into a tight fist and blood was oozing through the cracks of the pressed together fingers. Crimson droplets fell to the dusty ground to form ugly brown stains.

Down at the base of the natural crater among the hills, a few steers snorted and scratched nervously at the cropped pasture.

Barney Tait, who had ridden halfway up the slope, jerked his horse to a halt and snapped his head around to rake angry and fearful eyes over the unsettled herd.

"What the hell?" O'Brian croaked to shatter the shocked silence clamped over the men in front of the ranch house.

All of them followed the direction of his furious gaze to locate Edge, who still stood at the fence, the Winchester resting across the top bar. "Mistakes happen," the unexpressive half-breed responded to the spoken question and the tacit curiosity.

"Mistake?" the sheriff blustered.

"He made it." A nod toward the scar-faced man dripping blood from his holed palm. "He called Mexicans greasers. He shouldn't have done that."

"Damnit, they didn't give a shit about it!" the injured cowhand snarled.

"They got other things to worry about," Edge replied evenly as he canted the rifle up to his shoulders. "I ain't."

"You have now, mister!" the man countered. He sucked blood from his fist and spat it at the ground. "I ain't the kind to forget somethin' like this!"

He splayed his fingers to exhibit the blood-oozing hole through his palm.

Edge nodded impassively while others eyed the wound with disgust. "You catch on fast, feller. These *vaqueros* are Mexicans. Same as my pa was. Figured I'd give you a hand to remember that."

The cattle had calmed and Barney Tait was

completing his ride up the slope, chewing angrily on a wad of tobacco.

"What crazy fool fired off a gun and spooked the critters?" he yelled as he closed with the group.

"That crazy fool!" O'Brian taunted with a curt nod at Edge. "He might be a real hot-shot gunslinger, Tait. But you got a lot to teach him about how to act around a herd of cows this big!"

"Take it easy, Barney," Taggart placated as the Big-T foreman reined in his horse and glowered at Edge. "There's been no harm done."

"There's been harm done!" the scar-faced man growled, waving his injured hand. He transferred his anger from Edge to O'Brian. "You gonna let him get away with this, Sheriff?"

"You were warned you were trespassing, Edwards!" Oscar Taggart snapped. "All you men get the same warning. If you leave right now I'll guarantee you safe conduct off the Big-T."

"We're leaving!" Saxby growled, moving his intense stare from Edge to Taggart to Tait and to the *vaqueros*. "And you've been given fair warning. The other side of the county line you'll have to fight for every inch you try to drive those cows!"

His spurs jabbed his horse forward and the other cowhands were quick to follow. Only Edwards spared time for a backward glance, his eyes filled with hate for the man who had blasted a hole in his hand.

The four deputies waited eagerly for O'Brian's order to move out. The *vaqueros* tacitly implored him to remain, but he shook his head as the lines of sourness in his sun-darkened skin seemed to deepen.

"Saxby told you like it is. Up to you boys. For what it's worth, I wouldn't ride for the Big-T outfit for a thousand bucks a week." He shifted his gaze to insure that Taggart, Tait and the half-breed saw the full

57

measure of his loathing for them. "This whole thing makes me sick to my stomach!"

Edge moved to his gelding and pushed the Winchester back into the boot. "So take a powder."

Chapter Six

THE bunkhouse of the Big-T ranch had cots for twenty men but Edge had the place to himself for what remained of the hot afternoon. He entered the long, narrow, low-ceilinged room after stabling his horse. He was not surprised to discover that, in relative terms, the animal was enjoying better creature comforts than he was. For he had already seen that Tait had a higher regard for stock than for men, and that Oscar Taggart's sole concern with his spread was that it should produce the highest return for the lowest investment.

But, even so, the half-breed relished the feel of the lumpy mattress on the hard boards beneath his back as he lay on the cot and listened to the sounds of men and animals outside. For he had not had access to the simple luxury of any sort of bed, except for his blankets on the parched earth of Mexico, since he rode out of San Parral. And that had been many weeks ago. Just how many scorching days and bitterly cold nights had passed since then, he was not sure. Enough, though, for him to be certain that he had accepted the brutal death of Isabella Montez with ice-cold resignation—despite the miles he had traveled and the men he had killed in the vain attempt to possess her.

So the sadness that the boy at the cantina had detected in the lone stranger was not a sign of fading grief. Rather, it was a response to the now-certain knowledge that the man was unable to experience grief. For if he

59

was denied that deepest of emotions surely he had been drained of the capacity to feel lesser human reactions to the events triggered by his presence.

Since his accidental shot had shattered Jamie's life, he had always insulated himself against emotional involvement in circumstances outside his control. Then, when the death of his parents made survival entirely his own responsibility, he had begun to build a defense against being affected by the consequences of personal conflicts.

He had never regarded himself as different from other men in this respect, accepting this hardening process as a necessary step along the way from adolescence into adulthood.

During the war it had been essential for every man engaged on the field of battle to possess such a defense against the evils of human cruelty. For then, a certain way to violent death was to pause in futile reflection on tragedy that had already occurred.

The peace that followed was to be more harrowing than war for this man; and he survived it, in large part, because of his impassiveness to the death and destruction which continually dogged his tracks or lurked ahead on the trail he followed.

But, until he turned on that dusty street in San Parral and saw the inert, blood-stained corpse of Isabella Montez, his defense against dangerous emotion had been only a shield—a skin deep veneer for the benefit of others. Behind this he had suffered whatever brand of mental torment his cruel fate had decreed for him.

It had become easier to bear since he overcame his grief at losing Beth Day—for he made a conscious effort to remain apart from his fellow human beings, in contact with them but inviting no warmth into the relationships. There had been occasions when he thought he was completely free of any sort of punishment that went beyond the physical. But when his resolve weakened so that he felt an affinity with somebody, he was always proved wrong. Tragedy inevitably struck and the familiar pain assaulted his mind. But each time with less intensity.

Now it was finished. He could never be made to suffer mental anguish again. And on the ride from San Parral to the cow town on the Mexican side of the Rio Grande he had come to terms with this—venturing close to the border line of self-pity. For, in beating fate's decree that he should suffer for every step he took along his trail of violence, he felt he had become less of a man. *As cold as a Sierra Madre night,* the old Mexican had called him. Always he had sought to appear this way.

There was no longer any need for pretense.

"You wish food, *señor?*"

Edge had not slept through the afternoon. He had simply sprawled out on his back on the cot closest to the door of the spartanly furnished bunkhouse, his right hand close to the Remington in his holster and his left just a few inches from where the stock of the Winchester jutted out of his gear piled on the floor. His hat was tipped forward over his forehead, but his eyes remained open—idly watching the changing pattern of light and shade on the walls and ceiling as the sun crawled down the western sky.

It was the old-timer who spoke from the threshold. A small man of no more than five feet, with crinkled features and a sparse body. Almost bald but with a thick moustache. His dirty white shirt was spotted with grease marks and the bandana that now hung from his belt was damp from mopping sweat. He was holding a tin plate heaped high with beef and beans.

"Taste as good as it smells?" Edge asked, folding up and swinging his feet to the floor.

"I have cooked thousands of meals on hundreds of

trails in Mexico and the United States. The drovers they always complain because that is their way. But never have I been fired."

"Obliged," the half-breed said, thrusting out a hand.

The cook advanced into the bunkhouse and surrendered the plate of food. Edge delved into his gear for his own eating implements.

"Everybody stay?"

Saxby and his men and the sheriff and deputies had still been in sight when the half-breed led his horse into the stable block. The *vaqueros* had been watching the departing riders enviously, while Oscar Taggart and Barney Tait issued tacit challenges for the Mexicans to follow suit. Then, when Edge walked from the stable to the bunkhouse, the owner of the Big-T had been countering Saxby's threat of unemployment—warning the hapless *vaqueros* that he had more influence than the spread's former top hand and promising he would use it if the men broke their contract with him.

Reasoning that he would learn the outcome sooner or later, Edge had made no attempt to eavesdrop on Taggart's speech or the responses it drew. He had listened only to the sound of voices, then the clop of hooves and slap of harness as trail-weary horses were urged into movement. After that, the loudest sound that reached the quiet bunkhouse was the lowing of cattle in the basin below the ranch buildings, until advancing footfalls on the hard-packed dirt of the yard signaled the approach of the cook.

"*Si, señor,*" the little old man replied. "It was allowed we should discuss the position and we did this. And agreed one job is better than no job. Especially a job such as this one. The money we earn will last a very long time in Mexico. Long enough for people to forget how we earned it."

Edge nodded, then swallowed hurriedly as the cook

made to leave the bunkhouse. "Glad to have you along, feller. What's your name?"

"Pancho, *señor*. Something else you should know of me. I think. I despise the kind of man you are."

The half-breed was chewing food, and spoke around it. "Should that worry me, Pancho?"

A shake of the head, the expression regretful. "I can cause you no harm, *Señor* Edge. But it will be my pleasure to dig your grave should this be necessary. For Don Camilo and Don Jorge who were fine men. And for the storekeeper and his *señora*."

"I ain't known for spreading happiness, feller," the half-breed said, moving the old man to anger by his easy acceptance of the hatred.

"Your kind of man is good for . . ."

"So dig a deep grave."

Pancho was puzzled.

"And pack the dirt real well. It's hard to keep a good man down."

Edge was weary of Pancho's helpless enmity toward him. He brought an end to the exchange with a brief, ice-cold stare through glinting blue slits in the shade of the hat brim. The old man's response was a fast and unsteady whirl and a vicious slam of the door. Then Edge continued with the meal, plain, plentiful and well cooked. He listened to Barney Tait talking with Pancho out in the sun-drenched yard. Again he failed to catch the words being spoken, but detected in the tones of the men that questions were being asked and answered. Then the door opened wide enough for the Big-T foreman to thrust his head inside.

"The cook tells me you know we've still got an outfit. We'll be headin' out with the critters at sun-up tomorrow."

Edge nodded.

Tait seemed about to withdraw, then halted the move. "Oh, yeah. More critters there are in a bunch, the harder they are to control. We got five thousand cows down there. Any loud noise they don't expect is liable to send them runnin' every which way."

Another nod from the man eating the beef and beans. "Makes cows like some people then, uh?"

"What's that supposed to mean?"

Edge set his empty plate down on the floor and stretched out again on the lumpy mattress. "Don't like being in crowds, feller."

Tait scowled and slammed the door with greater force than Pancho had used. The footfalls of the Big-T foreman stomped on the yard, then became merged with many other sounds as the *vaqueros* not engaged in watching the herd gathered for the evening meal.

Edge slept, resting just below the level of consciousness. Dreamlessly. On occasions he was brought close to waking as the Mexicans bedded down for the night or came and went as the guard on the herd changed during the dark hours. But there was no threat of danger from the embittered men who entered and left the bunkhouse with a minimum of noise. They did not talk, and if they paid any attention to the sleeping half-breed it was simply to glance at him fearfully, secretly apportioning to him a large share of the blame for their predicament.

He awoke an hour before sunrise, to the pleasant aroma of cooking food that infiltrated into the bunkhouse through cracked timbers and broken windows, carried on the cold morning air. When he hauled his gear outside, the early hours' air was colder, damp with dew. Dark wood smoke rose from a stack in the cookhouse roof, rising high in a seemingly solid column toward the star-pricked blackness of the sky. A kerosene lamp burned dimly and a range glowed brightly behing two windows of the cookhouse. Elsewhere the ranch buildings were in total darkness. At the foot of the basin the herd was still bedded down under the sullenly watchful eyes of the four slow-riding sentries.

In the stable, crowded and sweet smelling with the horses of the off-duty men, the half-breed stripped himself naked—revealing to the disinterested gaze of the animals the hard, muscular leanness of a body liberally scattered with scars.

Cold was a familiar discomfort and he accepted stoically its touch on his undraped flesh. He vented only a low grunt through clenched teeth as he lowered himself into the brimful horse trough, then worked vigorously with a cake of soap to remove old sweat and trail dust from his pores. When his skin was clean, he used the razor from the neck pouch to scrape the bristles from his cheeks, jaw and throat. He had no need of a mirror to stop the blade short at the mustache and the long sideburns that reached far below the level of his earlobes under the thick fall of his hair.

He was fully dressed again, and had drained and refilled the trough with fresh water, when footfalls sounded on the yard outside. And the bunkhouse door was kicked open.

"All right, you men!" Barney Tait snarled. "Outta the sack and get some grub! Time to start earnin' your pay!"

The half-breed began to saddle his gelding as groans and curses greeted the Big-T foreman's raucous words.

"Where the hell's Edge?" Tait sounded at once angry and afraid.

There was no response from the bunkhouse.

"I saw him go to the stable, *señor*," Pancho supplied from the other side of the yard.

"Feed everyone. Includin' the men down at the herd. Then get the chuck wagon ready to leave. You men attend to your horses soon as you've eaten. We ain't got no . . ."

"*Señor* Tait!" a *vaquero* cut in calmly.

"What you want?"

"We have been on many drives. We know what to do."

"So friggin' do it!" the foreman retorted. "And do it quick!"

He had been crossing to the stable as he yelled his ill-tempered orders. As he issued the final one he jerked open the door and stared at Edge with undisguised surprise.

"Neat and clean as a new pin," he drawled after the half-breed had straightened from cinching the saddle to the gelding's belly, and nodded a greeting.

"Ain't that allowed on a cattle drive, feller?" Edge countered as he lashed his bedroll behind the saddle.

Tait was unshaven and still stained with yesterday's dirt. He dug a plug of tobacco from a shirt pocket and bit off a chew. "Just one rule covers drivin' a herd of critters, mister. No matter what else happens, the cows come first."

The half-breed coaxed the gelding out of the stall and led him across the stable. "Obliged for the information. I'll be sure to watch where I'm treading."

Tait scowled and stood aside to allow Edge and the horse out into the yard. Then he spat some tobacco juice at the ground and went into the stable to attend to his own mount.

There was just a wisp of smoke from the stack on the cookhouse roof now. The lamp was out and the fireglow almost gone. Above the eastern horizon the stars were fading into infinity under the advance of gray dawn. In the yard, a line of bleary-eyed Mexicans moved into and out of the cookhouse, having their empty plates and mugs filled by Pancho and carrying them back to the bunkhouse. Some of them cast envious glances toward the freshly washed-up and shaved Edge as he mounted the gelding and rode across the

66

yard. Others looked at him with something akin to scorn.

He ignored them as he joined the end of the line, still astride the horse. When he reached the doorway he dug out a mug from inside his bedroll and leaned down to thrust it toward Pancho.

"Just coffee, feller."

"It is bad to start a day's work with a belly that is empty," the almost bald old-timer advised as he carried the coffee pot to the door and tilted it over the extended mug.

"You sound like my ma used to."

"But now you are old enough to know your own mind?"

"Maybe," Edge allowed, and sipped the hot, strong coffee as he watched Barney Tait lead his stallion from the stable, mount up and ride through the open gateway.

"And not to like what you have become, I think?"

"You're a good cook and you make fine coffee, feller. Stick to what you know best."

"*Si, señor.* But a man cannot help what he thinks. And an old man like I am . . . he has behind him the years to make his advice good. Give Taggart back his money and leave."

Edge sipped the scalding coffee, draping his free hand on the saddlehorn. "My ma gave me advice because she loved me, feller."

A sad-faced nod. "*Si.* That is one of the things mothers are for. I offer it because I have regard for those *hombres.*" He waved a hand toward the bunkhouse. "I think that if you leave, they will have the courage to go." He sighed and shrugged. "But you will do only what is to your own advantage. So I am wasting my time, am I not?"

"I owe nothing to you or to the *vaqueros,*" the half-breed pointed out.

"Nor to anybody who does not pay you?" He sighed again as he turned and went back toward the range. "I tried, even though I knew I was bound to fail."

"Know the feeling, feller," Edge replied softly, and tipped the coffee dregs out of his mug before he stowed it back into his bedroll. "I do that all the time."

He tugged on the reins to turn the gelding and then heeled him forward across the yard and out of the gateway. Behind him, the Taggart father and son emerged from the ranch house, washed and shaved, smiling in anticipation of breakfast. As four disheveled but already fed *vaqueros* headed for the stables.

Down in the basin Tait was circling the herd alone, having signaled the quartet of Mexicans to head up the hill to eat. They closed with the half-breed at a midway point on the slope between the ranch buildings and the steers. The forty-year-old, broad-shouldered and barrel-chested man with two front teeth missing—who was obviously the top hand among the Mexicans—gave a grim-faced nod as he and the others reined in their mounts.

"Do something for you?" Edge asked.

"Pancho the cook, he has spoken with you?"

"A couple of times. Once to tell me he'd like to bury me. Then he said I should leave."

The man pushed his tongue into the gap where his teeth had been, his dark eyes pondering a problem. The three *vaqueros* with him seemed anxious to ride on as the relief guards came out of the yard. "You will not do this because, I think, in your own way you are as honorable as we are, *señor*. You have accepted money and put your name to a contract. I said this when we talked while you slept."

"What are you saying now, feller?"

"That we have all made a bad mistake. Because we were greedy for money. But men must learn to live with their mistakes. We will ride for the Big-T as long

68

as you do, *Señor* Edge. And if there is trouble, you will tell us what to do. We will not be like helpless children—as we were when the *gringo* insulted all Mexicans." He smiled his pleasure at having spoken his piece. The other three were still unhappy. "My name is Luis Lacalle and my word is my bond."

He extended his right hand and leaned to the side. Edge accepted the handshake and noticed that the quartet of guards riding by were as sullen-faced as three of the men they were relieving.

"Glad to know I can rely on you, feller," the half-breed acknowledged.

"On all of us!" Lacalle growled, treating his fellow countrymen to a scowl. "But some of us take longer than others to recover from our mistakes."

Edge nodded and heeded his gelding forward. He rode slowly in the wake of the four new guards as Lacalle and the other three continued on up the slope to the ranch house.

Tait had completed a circuit of the perimeter fence to check the stock and now he sat in a relaxed attitude astride his stationary stallion, contentedly chewing on his wad of tobacco as he watched the enormous herd of longhorns. Just as had happened the previous afternoon, the Big-T foreman's bad humor had been soothed out of him by contact with the cattle.

But he was moved to glowering bad temper again by the half-breed's approach. "Lacalle tell you I've made him top hand?"

"No, feller. But I figure you made a good choice."

"What was the hand shakin' all about?"

"His idea. Gave me his word he and the rest of them will make the best of a lousy job."

"Damnit, you ain't the boss around here!" Tait snarled.

"Never made no claims, feller. You heading the herd due north from here?"

Tait shot a sour glance up the slope. "Just as soon as them sonsofbitches move their asses down here to start work." He snapped his head around as Edge urged his horse into movement. "Hey, where you goin'?"

"Break that rule you told me about. The herd has to come after me if I check on what's ahead."

"Take us till midday to reach the county line, mister. And there won't be no trouble from Saxby before that. Weren't no, hand-shakin', but when O'Brian makes a promise, he keeps it. So best you stay with the herd. Learn how to handle this many critters on the move while there ain't nothin' else to worry about."

Edge looked back over his shoulder. "If Taggart had wanted me to herd cattle, feller," he said as the gelding continued to carry him away from the glowering Tait, "he'd be paying me a hundred a week. He figures I rate higher than that and I figure a man deserves value for his money."

"That don't mean you gotta go lookin' for trouble where there ain't any, damnit!" Tait snarled.

The half-breed ignored the angry words as he reached the low point of the basin and started to swing the gelding to the left, heading him around the outside of the barbed wire fence enclosing the longhorns. The entire sky was gray now, all the stars dimmed into nothingness and the quarter moon reduced to just a pale crescent above the southern arc of hills. The air had altered from cold to cool and the brightening area above the eastern horizon promised a comforting warmth that would precede long hours of harsh heat.

The massed steers accepted the half-breed indifferently, some of the animals on the fringe of the herd not even interrupting their grazing when he rode past at an easy pace. He came close to two of the *vaqueros* as he swung around the western side of the fence and acknowledged their grim-faced nods with a brief raising of his hand.

Then, as the first yellow shaft of sunlight lanced down into the basin from a gap between two hilltops, he rode away from the cattle and the men whose job it was to handle them, heading up the slope of the northern curve of hills into country that appeared devoid of all human presence save his own. And he at once experienced a lightening of his mood—which was the first indication he had that he had been infected by the aura of gloom and discontent that prevailed at the ranch behind him.

He found the knowledge vaguely disconcerting, for it meant that he had not become entirely a new man during that violence-shattered day in San Parral. He could still be made to feel the burden of responsibility that others elected for him to carry—or paid him to accept.

But out in the silent and uncrowded open country he was his own man: self-confidently conscious of what he had to do and relishing the freedom of action he possessed.

So he rode easy in the saddle over the crest of the hill and maintained a relaxed, involuntary watch on the features of the broad valley stretching out ahead of him. The warm air of sunrise was clean, untainted by the odors of men unaware of their destinies and animals doomed to die in a short while.

Life was not good for the man called Edge, but at a time such as this it was the best he could ever expect.

Death brushed him two hours later.

He was four miles beyond the boundary of the Big-T spread by then, having crossed on to public land through a broad gap in the fence, which had been enlarged from a conventional gateway so that the massive herd of longhorns could be driven north without delay. The sun was high and hot enough to create a haze along every horizon and the Big-T pasture had given way to an arid terrain of convoluted ridges of rock with depressions of dusty soil between.

71

Edge was riding northwest along such a ridge, flanking the only trench broad enough to take the large herd, when he glimpsed a flash of sunlight off metal. The brief glint showed at the top of the slightly lower ridge a quarter mile to his right. Then, as he snapped his head around to get a firmer bearing on the position, it was pinpointed by a puff of white muzzle smoke.

He had wheeled the gelding and plunged him down the slope on the blind side of the ridge when the report of the rifle shot cracked against his eardrums. But Edge's head and back were still exposed and the bullet came close enough to him for him to feel the disturbed air of its slipstream rush across the flesh of his neck.

Horse and rider were out of sight, the gelding snorting with panic as his hooves slithered on loose shale, when the second shot cracked. The sound was simultaneous with the thud of the bullet into rock.

Edge fought for control of the terrified animal with the skillful use of the reins and his heels. But the onus was on the gelding to beat his own fear—to bend and straighten his legs at the right moments to take account of degree of slope and treacherous movement of the surface under its hooves. The half-breed could do little more than stay in the saddle and stirrups as the downward plunge continued, his lips sealed over the urge to snarl obscenities and eyes cracked against the billowing dust.

For more than twenty feet there was a danger that rider and horse would be flung to the cascading rocks with their dust-veiled threat to shattered limbs. But then the gelding responded to the calming influence of the man, bending his hindlegs to slope his back into the hill and using his rigid forelegs as a brake to the downslide.

The momentum slackened, then suddenly stopped.

Pieces of shale continued to skitter downward. But not for long. All sound except for the breathing of Edge and the horse was silenced. The dust settled. The eyes of the gelding ceased to bulge and the half-breed began again to sweat at the normal rate.

"Easy, feller," Edge said, soft and soothing when the horse snickered as he made the first move to dismount. When he was himself standing on the treacherous shale, he stroked the animal's neck. "Figure to make him pay for trying to upset us."

Careful of where he trod and constantly watching the unsafe ground in front of the animal, he slowly led his mount to the foot of the slope. It was a narrow stretch of parched and dusty earth with a solid but steeper rise on the other side. There were no trees or brush to which he could hitch the horse, but it had been a long ride from San Parral and Edge had used part of the time to train his mount. So it was sufficient for him to hang the reins forward to the ground—and when he moved away after sliding the Winchester from the boot, the animal remained stock still.

Edge went back up the slopes as carefully as he had descended the second half—but on a long, diagonal line that brought him to the crest some two hundred feet left of where he had been a target for the sharp-shooter. He gave the man credit for not being a fool and he removed his hat and made use of morning sun shadow to chance a look across the quarter-mile-wide valley.

Nothing moved on the opposite ridge and there was no rifle barrel in position for the sun to glint on. He waited a few moments and made another fast survey. Longer than the first because this time his coldly glinting eyes raked over the intervening low ground as well as the ridge.

A black shadow moved across white rock, but it was cast by a buzzard that swooped low through the hot air above the arid land, then spiraled high with a croak of disappointment.

"Stick around," the half-breed murmured as he settled into a comfortable sitting position on the shale, watching the scavenger as it found the effortless rise of a thermal, and pumping the action of the rifle. "Up to the feller across the way whether you'll get late breakfast or an early lunch."

Edge was as patient and unmoving as the gelding below him. He had his hat back on now to shade his head from the strengthening heat of the sun and in the shadow of its broad brim the lines of his dusty and sweaty face were as relaxed as if he were asleep. In fact, his eyes were closed so that he could concentrate all his attention on the sense of hearing.

Only occasionally did he crack open the hooded lids to check on the passage of time from the sluggish movement of his own shadow. After an hour had slid silently into history, he rechecked the eastward view from the top of the ridge.

The man who had tried to kill him was the scarfaced Edwards, whose curiosity had negated cautious patience. When Edge first saw him, he was halfway down the slope, the barrel of his rifle swinging to and fro at the same nervous tempo as his moving head. The half-breed saw him for only a part of a second, but there could be no mistake about his identity. For the right hand fisted around the barrel of the Winchester was wrapped in a blood-stained and dirt-streaked bandage.

Edge resumed his previous position, eyes closed and hearing strained to pick up the first sound of Edwards's approach. And the hot morning silence was scratched by footfalls on rock. It was counterpointed a few moments later by the rasping of labored breathing—perhaps caused by exertion or, more likely, the tension of fear.

The half-breed's face was abruptly no longer in repose. The slits of his eyes glinted like slivers of blue glass and his thin lips curled back to reveal the whiteness of his teeth in a cold grin of evil intent. He remained seated on the shale, but turned his head and nestled the stock plate of the Winchester against his shoulders. His eyes and the muzzle of the rifle became fixed on a point a hundred feet along the ridge where he was certain Edwards would appear.

The footfalls faltered and the man cursed at his near stumble. Edge took first pressure against the trigger of the rifle.

From the south came a sound like far-off thunder—except that no thunder roll ever lasted so long. It was the beat of cloven hooves against the sun-baked earth of Texas as five thousand head of cattle moved north.

The noise got louder by the moment and Edge could no longer rely on his hearing to signal the moves made by his would-be killer. But he had already pinpointed Edwards's position. And when he triggered a shot he heard the man's shrill cry of alarm.

Before the chips of rock exploded by the impact of the bullet had completed their flight, Edge had powered upright. Then he sent shale showering down his side of the slope from under his pumping feet. He reached the high point of the ridge in moments, another shell already levered into the breech of the Winchester.

Despite the swelling volume of sound from the approaching herd, Edwards heard the clatter of skittering rock pieces. But he was still recovering from the shock of the unexpected shot and was driven into deeper fear by the sudden appearance of his prey become predator.

Edge literally leapt into view, using the first patch of firm ground under his feet to power himself into a jump. And, as he landed—in full view of the man who was belly down on the slope a hundred feet away—the Winchester exploded a second shot. This bullet also hit rock, but there was pain as well as fear in the shrill sound vented from Edwards's gaping mouth. For the broken fragments rained into his face to spot it with droplets of blood.

"Jesus!" he shrieked, the blasphemy a continuation of his strident scream.

Edge shook his head as he pumped the rifle's lever action. "You missed me, feller. I just rose up from the other side of the hill. Let go of the gun."

Edwards was holding the Winchester by the frame in his uninjured hand, on the far side of his trembling body from where Edge covered him. Just for a moment, his face showed he was considering a desperate attempt to roll and explode a shot. But when the half-breed stepped toward him, rifle in a rock-steady aim on the center of his blood-run face, he loosened his grip. The surrendered Winchester slithered twenty feet down the slope before its stock was halted by a hollow.

"You're gonna kill me?" Edwards accused, almost choking as he tried to work saliva into his fear-parched throat.

"You should have been that smart earlier, feller," Edge replied, closing in on the helpless cowhand. "You want to get on your feet?"

"It was Saxby's idea, mister," Edwards blurted, trying to control his quaking as he rose onto all fours and then pushed himself erect.

"He own you?" the half-breed asked, coming to a halt when the Winchester muzzle was three inches from the cowhand's chest.

"No! But he knew I had good reason to be mad at you. After you put a hole through my hand. We got to drinkin' last night. In town. Just a few of us that was out at the Big-T. He wanted us all to ride against your whole outfit. But the others, they didn't want no part of any shoot out."

76

Edwards was still shaking badly, unable to wrench his terrified gaze away from the fixed cold stare of the half-breed's eyes. But the way his voice rose had nothing to do with his fear. He had to shout to make himself heard above the noise of the herd. They were below and behind him, moving steadily between the slopes of the high ground under a cloud of dust and flies.

"But you were happy to do a little bushwhacking for him, uh?" Edge yelled.

The man knew he was doomed. And although his limbs and shoulders continued to quake a physical response to his mental anguish, his blood-caked face became set in an expression of grim defiance. "Sure I was!" he roared, and held up his shaking right hand with its filthy dressing. "Any man who'll blast a hole in somebody just because of a wrong word—I'd kill him with pleasure! I thought that when I was drunk last night. And I didn't have no second thoughts about it while I was waitin' for you this mornin'."

Edge allowed him to finish, as the point rider broke away from the relentlessly moving herd of longhorns to gallop his horse across the slope.

"Just you and Saxby, feller? In a while only Saxby?"

"Don't count on it, you sonofabitch! Them that didn't want any part of a shoot out ain't ready to leave it there. They left their guns in the holsters, but they dug deep into their pockets. Matt's halfway to San Antonio by now. With plenty of cash to hire the best guns in Texas!"

Barney Tait brought his black stallion to a skidding, snorting halt. Edwards was at last able to tear his gaze away from the trap of the half-breed's stare—to look up into the fury coming from the face of the new arrival.

"He's gonna kill me, Mr. Tait!"

"Not with that rifle, he ain't!" the Big-T foreman

77

snarled, shifting his blazing eyes from Edwards to Edge and then down to where the herd was tramping noisily past.

But a movement on the periphery of his vision caused him to snap his head around. In time to see Edge's right hand leave the Winchester barrel and disappear momentarily into the long hair at the nape of his neck. When it re-emerged it was wrapped around the handle of the razor which Tait had good reason to remember.

The half-breed's arm straightened as he leaned forward from the waist, over the length of the Winchester still aimed one-handed at Edwards's heart.

The scar-faced man with fresh blood drying on his face had time to start a scream as the defiance was swept from his features by sheer terror. And a final tremor quaked him from head to toe as he glimpsed the sun-glinting blade of the razor.

Then the blade dug into his flesh, an inch below his left ear—and was slashed in a ripping arc across his throat, to come clear close to his right ear lobe.

A crimson torrent erupted from the gaping wound. And his dying scream faded into a meek gurgle as his windpipe became awash with blood. His hands reached out for support and found the aimed rifle. They gripped it for perhaps a full second. Edge angled the Winchester down at the ground and Edwards dropped hard to his knees. The man was feeling no pain. Just terror of what awaited him beyond death. Then he knew the awesome secret, releasing his grip and collapsing onto his side. His wide eyes stared, fixed and vacant, at the slow moving herd and the men controlling the longhorns. His gaping mouth filled with blood and just a few drops spilled over to run down his chin.

The half-breed stooped to wipe the razor clean on its new victim's shirt before he replaced it in the neck pouch.

"That's the most brutal friggin' thing I ever did see!" Barney Tait rasped. "He didn't have a chance!"

Edge eased the rifle hammer to the rest and canted the weapon to his shoulder. "He was standing there trembling like a Colorado aspen for a couple of minutes, feller," he replied dispassionately.

The man astride the horse chewed vigorously on his wad of tobacco. "I don't give a damn about . . ."

"Seems to me," Edge cut in, turning to start over the ridge where his gelding waited, "that I gave him a fair shake."

Chapter Seven

NOBODY asked Edge for an explanation of the events leading up to the killing of Edwards and he did not offer one. And by the evening of the fourth day out from the Big-T ranch, the men who witnessed the bloodletting on the sun-drenched ridge had been drained of any feeling about what they had seen.

It was only at night that they had an opportunity to make these feelings known to the half-breed. For during the daylight hours when the herd was moving inexorably northward—following a route to pick up the Goodnight-Loving Trail west of Fort Concho—Edge rode out ahead, or occasionally swept wide around behind the herd to check for the possibility of trouble to the south, east and west. Thus, he only came into close contact with the drovers at night camp during the eating of the meal cooked by Pancho and the bedding down to rest. At the first camp, the Taggarts, Tait and the Mexicans made an emphatic point of avoiding him—speaking to him only when it was strictly necessary and most of the time acting as if he was not present. He knew they were afraid of him.

The next night the men had overcome their fear of him and he sensed their scorn as they watched him attend to his horse, eat his food and bed down.

Finally, there was curiosity with undertones of nervousness and contempt. On several occasions during that night—at the campfire beside the parked chuck wagon and when he made one of his periodic patrols around the bedded down steers—men came close to posing questions to him. But each time they were dissuaded by his icy gaze and grimly set mouthline.

By the end of the fourth day the men had lost interest in Edge and his cold-blooded brutality on the ridge. For by this time the killing seemed to them like something from ancient history. Bone-deep weariness of the drive was beginning to take its toll on the drovers. And they had another man to hate and fear, for more personal reasons.

Tait was a hard and dedicated trail boss whose preference for cattle above men became more evident over every mile of Texas that was put behind the massive herd. The longhorns were in prime condition and ever eager to push on from dawn to dusk in the wake of the big lead steer. The *vaqueros* were skilled at their trade, but subject to human weaknesses. As an outfit they were undermanned to cope with such a large herd. During the day they were constantly in the saddle, riding at point, swing, flank or drag. Eating dust and sweating under the harsh blaze of the sun. At night it seemed to a resting man that he had been asleep for only a few minutes before he was roused to take his duty as guard.

None of them had expected the job to be easy, irrespective of the high pay for the additional risks involved in driving the hated Big-T herd. For pushing any herd up any trail was an exhausting, uncomfortable, dirty chore. But this was a real bad one, because the trail boss demanded twenty miles a day despite his lack of manpower, which was double the daily distance covered by most herds on the trail.

It was inevitable that the frenetic pace would affect the men and Edge saw the first sign of strain at that fourth night camp.

The herd was bedded down in a broad grassy valley

featured with rock outcrops and criss-crossed by numerous gullies. It was a fine, clear night and the men on guard and those eating Pancho's beef stew and sourdough bread turned their faces eagerly toward a light, cool breeze wafting down the valley from the north. But with their hunger satisfied and the sweat of the hot day dried on their filthy flesh, the *vaqueros* began to brood about their lot.

As always, Edge sat apart from the other members of the outfit, impassively smoking a cigarette and drinking coffee—his back against a wheel of the chuck wagon into which Pancho was packing his cooking utensils. Oscar and Zeke Taggart were already unfurling their bedrolls close to the roped remuda of horses, the son as exhausted as the father from the long days of dusty heat behind the herd. City men, they were unaccustomed to watching for breakaway steers that had eluded the skillful but overstretched *vaqueros*.

Tait was out with the longhorns, taking the first night watch with three of the Mexicans. The other seven drovers—joined by the aged cook after he had packed away his pots—sat on their saddles in a group to one side of the fire. Smoking cheroots or pipes and talking softly in their own language.

But, the half-breed learned from the disjointed snatches of the conversation which carried to his disinterested ears, the talk was not about himself or his actions. And he was not being pointedly ostracized any longer. The men, with unshaven, work-weary faces—constantly shifting their postures to try to ease aching muscles—were exchanging examples of Tait's snarling deprecations of their work and rasping their discontent about every aspect of the job they had regretted taking almost from the very start.

Hearing them, and wrapping a blanket around his shoulders as the cooling breeze strengthened and got colder with the advance of evening into night, Edge briefly recalled occasions during the war when he had sat apart from the troopers under his command, aware of their discontented bellyaching which almost always resulted in him becoming the convenient subject of the resentment.

If he had felt anything for the troopers at such times—or the *vaqueros* now—it was mild scorn. Toward men who had chosen, or been drafted, to do a job and then indulged in futile complaints.

"*Señor* Taggart!" Luis Lacalle said sharply, rising to his feet.

"What do you want?" Zeke growled sleepily.

"Your father."

The younger Taggart folded up from his bedroll, red-eyed and haggard with fatigue. "He's asleep, mister. Which is what I want to be. If you've got a problem, see Tait."

He made to stretch out again, but the short, broadly built Lacalle stepped away from the group of tense-faced Mexicans toward him. "It is Mr. Tait who is our problem, *señor*. We wish to speak with the owner of the Big-T herd about this."

The man with gaps in his teeth had to make a considerable effort to be polite. Anger was brewing just beneath the surface of near exhaustion and he was determined not to be deterred from a course of action that had been difficult to decide upon.

Zeke recognized this and also saw that the men still seated by the breeze-fanned fire were as resolute as their spokesman. He seemed to recall the presence of the half-breed as an afterthought.

"Edge?"

"Yeah, feller?"

Zeke had been hardened by the first four days on the trail. This was easy to see in his general appearance—his flesh was as filthy as his new clothes and he

83

was unshaven, his once neatly kept hair now constantly disheveled. The redness of initial exposure to the sun had been shaded into brown. But all this merely contributed to a surface impression of the man—a temporary cover-up of the weak good looks that had seemed to stamp him as little more than a spoiled and callow youth at the outset. A more permanent change in him showed more subtle signs—in the way he had come to accept with grim stoicism the hardships of the trail; learning from his mistakes and becoming protective toward his father instead of having to rely on him and be resentful of the situation.

"You are hired to deal with trouble."

"From Saxby and whoever he can get to back him," Edge replied.

"*Señor* Edge cannot deal with this matter," Lacalle rasped, tense with impatience. "Your father is the owner of the cattle we drive. It is he who must be told we will go no farther unless . . ."

"You'll go all the way, feller," the half-breed interjected evenly. "Or stay right here. As buzzard meat."

"You cannot frighten us," the aged Pancho challenged as Lacalle expressed a sneer. "And you are not stupid, so you know this." He pointed an untrembling hand toward the cattle, a massive patch of darkness on the dusty pasture which appeared as white as northern snow in the moonlight. "Just the smallest of noises could start the *ganado* into a stampede. You know this. Mr. Tait told you, so you know."

Edge's face beneath his hat was as unmoving as his frame draped by the blanket. "Without drovers, I figure it won't make no difference whether the herd is quiet or running every which way, feller."

Lacalle's sneer became a scowl. "Twice you have said you will kill only men who help the one named Saxby. Only a moment ago . . ."

"Saxby aims to stop the Big-T herd getting to

Laramie. Back at the ranch there was a chance of hiring new hands. Out here if you and your bunch quit, you'll be doing just what Saxby wants."

Lacalle shook his head in a curt dismissal of the half-breed's argument. And swung to face the weary but resolute Zeke Taggart.

"One other thing, feller," Edge said before the Mexican could speak. "You gave your word to stick around so long as I stayed with the outfit. I figure a man who breaks his word ain't worth nothing more than a bullet."

Lacalle's anger broke surface as he whirled to glower at the calm, soft-spoken half-breed. "How can a man like you set store by honor?" he snarled. "A man who can cut the throat of another while he holds a gun on him? Such a man is not worthy of the word of Luis Lacalle!"

His voice was rising, louder and shriller. And as he shrieked his own name Oscar Taggart was wrenched out of sleep.

"What in tarnation is going on?" he demanded, shoving himself up into a sitting posture—and grimacing at the pains this triggered in aching muscles. He raked his bloodshot, heavily bagged eyes over the campsite. Then tried to fist the gritty feeling out from under the lids.

"The Mexicans want to quit, Dad," his son supplied.

"Like hell they will!" the elder Taggart roared, struggling to his feet. "Edge!"

The half-breed sighed. "We already did that bit, Mr. Taggart," he said. "We've reached the part where you either listen to Lacalle's whines or I blast him into a buzzard's breakfast."

"*Señor* Taggart!" the Mexicans' spokesman said quickly, struggling to contain his own anger as the owner of the Big-T herd was about to give full vent to

85

his. "All we ask for now is a hearing. Which will be as much in your interest as in ours."

"And if you listen, *señor*," Pancho augmented, "all you will lose is a few minutes sleep."

"Sleep's just about the most important thing we've got to lose right now," Zeke growled.

There was a tense pause in the exchange, the cold silence disturbed by the crackling of the fire and the contented lowing of cattle on the verge of sleep. Oscar Taggart looked from his exhausted son to the impassive Edge and then at Lacalle and the other Mexicans. And he sighed wearily in face of the *vaqueros*' determination not to be put off.

"All right," he allowed, then hurried on as Lacalle drew in a breath to begin voicing his grievances. "But I don't think you're going to tell me anything I don't already know. You're sick and tired of the way Barney Tait's been riding you. You've had enough of being yelled at to keep the herd moving faster than any herd ever traveled before. The outfit is only half as big as it should be and yet my foreman is acting as if we are at double strength. Is that about the size of it, Lacalle?"

The elder Taggart lacked the youthful flexibility of his son—and the burden of his sixty years made it physically impossible for him to combat the exhausting effects of the grueling pace of the drive. Like Zeke, he had been bronzed by the sun and dirtied by the dust, but his coloring seemed to emphasize the many deep lines of strain carved into his face. And the dirt ingrained in his pores, in combination with the gray bristles on his jowls and jaw, added to the impression of a man close to defeat. He looked thinner, shorter and much older than when the men had first seen him in the cantina of the town across the border.

But his voice and expression had a strength of character that counteracted his physical weakness and served notice on all those who might be ready to discount him. These were signs that, for as long as his body was able, he possessed the necessary determination to endure anything the trail demanded of him. And in his red-rimmed green eyes as he stared at the Mexicans there was bitter contempt for all who did not share his resolution.

"*Si, señor,*" Lacalle acknowledged, resentful of the scorn. "Even though you are paying us much money to . . ."

"I don't know one solitary thing about running a ranch, raising cattle or driving a herd," Oscar Taggart cut in, his tone rasping. "Only thing I know about this Big-T is that it's always given me a handsome profit. And I've got Barney Tait to thank for that. So whatever he does to get my cattle to Laramie is just fine with me." He looked into the blazing fire for a few moments and the sight of the leaping flames seemed to fuel his feeling against the *vaqueros*. He fixed Lacalle with another hard, unblinking glare. "Neither me nor my son are familiar with the rigors of trail driving. But we are prepared to take them without complaint. You and your men are supposed to be experienced . . ."

"*Señor!*" Lacalle snapped with a curt nod at the scowling Zeke. "You and he will make many thousands of dollars when the *ganado* are driven to Laramie. It is not the same!"

"If the herd gets to Laramie," Zeke corrected. "And if it gets there in ten weeks from the day we started out."

"Ten weeks!" Pancho gasped. "It cannot be done. One time I cook for Texas outfit who drive herd smaller than this from Brownsville to Cheyenne. This used up more than twenty weeks."

Oscar Taggart ignored both his son and the old-timer, but picked up the point they had made. "My foreman tells me it can be done!" he rasped at Lacalle. "And, as I told you before, I trust Barney Tait."

The first shot was a lonesome sound, isolated in a capsule of silence: the fire and the cattle subdued while the work-weary Mexicans assimilated this new aspect of the drive. But the silence after the crack of the fired rifle was much shorter than the one preceding it. For a man screamed in fear or pain as the loosed bullet tunneled through his flesh. And then five thousand head of cattle panicked in response to both sounds.

Even before the steers had pushed to their feet and the men at the camp had sprung erect, a burst of three more rifle shots exploded out in the cold darkness of night to the west of the spooked herd.

This trio of sharp cracks spurred livestock and men to greater speed.

The longhorns lunged into a thundering gallop as soon as they were four-footed, beginning a headlong race into the night, snorting their bovine terror.

The *vaqueros* responded automatically to the start of the stampede. The causes of their angry discontent were forgotten and they moved into action with smooth speed. They snatched up their saddles and ran for the remuda. Luis Lacalle had no need to issue orders for each man knew what to do. Cattle were their business and, as experienced trail hands, they acted without conscious thought to contain the dangers of a stampede.

"Go with them!" Oscar Taggart bellowed, after he and his son had used up almost a full minute in staring out at the moving mass of terrified cattle.

The Mexicans were galloping from the camp by then, spurs digging into flanks to demand flat-out speed from their mounts.

The old man looked first at his son, then swept his head to left and right in search of Edge. But the halfbreed was not immediately to be seen. The only other man left in camp was the cook.

"We are lucky, *señor*," Pancho said, having to raise

his voice hardly at all as the beat of steer and horse hooves diminished. "The stampede is away from us. It is bad when the *ganado* come toward the camp in their fear."

Taggart ignored the slow moving, quiet-spoken Mexican. He nodded his approval when he saw Zeke saddling a horse, clumsy in his haste. Then he spat out an obscenity as he at last spotted Edge. The half-breed was astride his saddled gelding and riding at a gallop—in the wrong direction. The herd and the men giving chase were racing northward along the valley. Edge rode a lonely route up a gully toward the high ground to the east.

"He's running out on us!"

"I do not think so, *Señor* Taggart," Pancho countered as he began to douse the fire. "There is a man who is totally evil except for one thing. He would risk his very life to keep his word."

The elderly owner of the Big-T looked set to snarl a rebuttal. But then bit back on the intended words and his gaunt face became wreathed in a frown as he saw the lone rider swing north just before he was skylined on the hill crest.

"I am sure he is ready to kill Luis Lacalle if the word that was given is broken," Pancho said flatly.

Edge was no more than a vague moving shadow against the hillside now. Then, after Taggart and the Mexican had shifted their gazes, they found it impossible to pinpoint man and horse again.

"Do you have any idea what he has in mind?"

Pancho shrugged his skinny shoulders. "A man like that continues to live only because he is able to hide his thoughts, *señor*. Just one thing is certain—that he does nothing without good reason."

"I'm ready, Dad," Zeke announced anxiously after he had swung astride his saddled stallion.

The herd and the drovers were now out of sight—

beyond the rise at the northern end of the valley. The dust of their momentum had settled and the sound of pumping hooves was lost in the distance.

"You will be no help, *señor*," Pancho advised. "You would be a hindrance even if you could catch up with the stampede."

"Stick to cooking, old man," Zeke growled.

"He's right, Ezekiel," the elder Taggart snapped. "Just a few minutes ago I admitted we're only passengers on this trip." He eyed the Mexican ruefully. "Unless somebody who knows trail herding has something for us to do."

"We must hitch the team to the wagon and then move on to where the herd has been halted, *señor*." He pointed up the valley to where the longhorns had been resting before the shot panicked them. "I heard a scream. Perhaps a man is wounded. Or dead. Somebody should go to see."

"Ezekiel!"

The younger Taggart did not like his appointed task. He was angry with Pancho for suggesting it, but complied sullenly with his father's order.

A hundred feet above the campsite and a quarter mile away from it, Edge saw Zeke Taggart heel the stallion forward and the two elderly men turn to go to where the wagon team cropped at tough grass.

The half-breed was back in the gully that he had followed almost to the top of the eastern high ground. But he was on foot now, having left his gelding in a deep hollow under the brow of the hill. He moved in a half crouch, cocked Winchester in a two-handed grip. And did not halt and fold down onto his haunches until he reached a low outcrop of rock at the side of the gully two hundred feet away from, and fifty feet above, the almost deserted camp.

Zeke Taggart was riding unhurriedly up the valley, ramrod straight with his head swinging this way and that. His attitude was that of a man afraid rather than one undertaking a simple chore.

And Edge knew that there was good reason for his fear—even if the city-bred man himself was aware only of an eerie sensation as he rode along through strange, night-shrouded country in search of another man who might be a corpse.

For all three men below where the half-breed was positioned were in danger of imminent death from another trio who were bellying down the final few feet of the western slope.

Edge had marked the general direction from which the first shot had come as he hurled aside his blanket and unfolded from against the wagon wheel. Then, as the cattle were spooked into noise and movement, his unblinking eyes had seen the muzzle flashes stabbed into the night by three more shots—short-lived spurts of brightness just below the crest of the western high ground.

As the dust of the stampede rose, to swirl in the cold air between the slopes, he had joined the *vaqueros* in racing for the huddle of unsettled horses. And been the first to saddle a mount, with the same smooth speed as the Mexicans but for a different purpose. For, just as their responses to the familiar dangers of a stampede were predetermined by experience, so his actions, after a malevolent burst of gunfire, were conditioned by events in his past.

And even had he known anything about overhauling the front-runners of a terrified herd of longhorns and turning them sharply to spiral in on the following animals, he would have ignored the steers. For in a situation such as this the man called Edge instinctively ignored the results of evil to strike at the cause.

From his vantage point on the rim of the hollow where his hard-breathing horse stood, he had ignored the group of *vaqueros* galloping into the dust cloud of

91

the stampede, and also ignored the stalled chuck wagon, depleted remuda and the three men who remained at the night camp. He crouched, as unmoving as the many outcrops of rock on the valley sides, peering across at the opposite slope, waiting with infinite patience for the merest hint of what the men who triggered the stampede intended to do. Not trying to outguess them, he had only one conviction in his cool, otherwise open mind—that if they showed themselves willing to pose a further threat to the Big-T trail drive, they were living on borrowed time.

They began their move down toward the night camp at a crouching run, just as Zeke Taggart rode away from the chuck wagon. The half-breed matched their cautious attitudes but made faster time, backtracking across the slope and then down the gully. He knew from the actions of the men that they were unaware of his presence in the valley. Swirling dust had obscured him when he galloped out of camp. And by the time the gritty motes had floated back to earth he was hidden against the hillside. As they themselves were, until they started down, relishing easy pickings as the main body of men galloped in pursuit of the runaway herd.

Close to the foot of the slope, the three men dropped from their crouches to go out full length. And stayed on their bellies as they started across level ground, rifles gripped in one hand, pushing through the dust and grass ahead of them. They ignored the rider sent in search of a casualty, devoting their concentrated attention to the pair of old-timers—Pancho hitching the team to the chuck wagon and Oscar Taggart loading up the gear and equipment left in the wake of the *vaqueros'* hurried departure. The American worked with awkward haste, the Mexican with measured slowness, neither revealing any sign that they suspected the stampede might have fatal consequences for themselves.

Edge rested the barrel of his Winchester across the top of a smooth rock and pressed his lips so tightly together they seemed to disappear. His bristled cheek made a tiny rasping sound against the stock of the rifle as he drew a bead on the back of one of the advancing trio. The sound, triggered by a slight movement of his curled forefinger, was much louder.

His victim arched off the ground and collapsed into total inertia.

The other two powered up onto their hands and knees with cries of alarm.

Pancho and the elder Taggart were shocked into statuelike representations of men in the act of hitching a team and loading a wagon. The American stared up toward Edge; the Mexican was held fascinated by the fresh corpse and the two living intruders.

"Dad!" Zeke Taggart howled. He had halted his horse to look down at the victim of the first shot to be fired by the intruders. Now he wrenched on the reins to wheel his horse.

His anguished cry echoed along with a second report from the half-breed's rifle, the bullet angling down, like the first, across the laden roof of the chuck wagon. It found its target in the gaping mouth of a man, the lips still drawn wide in the venting of shrill-voiced shock. The second corpse dropped into a prone position beside the first and the head seemed to swell. But this was only a trick of the moonlight—the torrent of blood from the wound spreading across the ground like an extension of the shadowed flesh from which it poured.

Another shot exploded while the half-breed was pumping the lever action of the Winchester. It had less power—fired by a revolver. But over a shorter range.

The surviving member of the trio was fully erect when the bullet drilled into his belly. He staggered backward on legs he seemed unable to control. Then he let go of his Winchester and was suddenly rock steady, his feet wide apart and both hands pressed to his wound. Blood oozed out from between his interlocked fingers. Fear contorted his face into an obscenely ugly mask.

"He's dead, Pancho!" Edge yelled, standing up from behind the outcrop as the Mexican made to explode another shot between the legs of the nervous horses.

"Dad! You all right, Dad?"

Zeke had galloped his horse back to camp and he pulled hard on the reins to bring the animal to a rearing, snorting halt beside the chuck wagon.

"They never got off a shot, son," his father replied shakily.

"He still looks alive to me, *señor*," Pancho croaked. He did not move as the team horses calmed and the half-breed came down the slope at a loping run. His arms remained outstretched, the gun in his fist covering the wounded man.

"Just a matter of time," Edge replied as he reached the rear of the chuck wagon and halted beside the Taggarts. Before he leveled the rifle at the terrified man, he clicked his thumb and forefinger together. "It can be like that. Or it could take hours. Maybe days."

The injured man licked his dry lips as the Mexican joined the three Americans. Like his dead partners he was in his mid-thirties. A tall, broad, hard man. Not the kind to beg for mercy. A man who had agreed to do a dangerous job and was prepared to accept the consequences if it went wrong. But not without fear.

"You can . . . finish me off with a bullet. Or . . . leave it with . . . just the one inside me."

"You're thinking straight, feller. Can you talk that way?"

"Go to hell!"

Edge angled the Winchester barrel downward and squeezed the trigger. The man's right ankle was shattered and he screamed as he crashed down, falling across the legs of one of the corpses. His frame jack-knifed and he writhed in a paroxysm of dual agonies as he clawed both sources of his pain.

Oscar Taggart and Pancho wrenched their shocked eyes away from the victim to stare at the unflinching profile of his impassive torturer. Zeke watched the agonized man with grim fascination.

"*Madre de Dios*," the Mexican gasped.

"You're not human!" the elder Taggart croaked.

"I'm what I am, feller. Which is what you wanted when you hired me." Edge nodded toward the twice-wounded man. "The same kind as him and his buddies. You found me and Saxby found them."

"He's right, Dad," Zeke said, his tone almost as dispassionate as that of the half-breed. He jerked a thumb up the valley. "I found one of the Mexicans out there. Maybe he was shot, or maybe he was thrown off his horse. There's no way to tell. He's been trampled by so many steers we won't know who he is until we see the rest. And these three men weren't coming down to help you break camp."

The injured man was groaning and whimpering now, after his agony had reached a high point and was subsiding. He lay on his side, curled up, his contorted face turned toward Zeke as the younger Taggart approached him, Colt drawn.

"What do you want to know, Mr. Edge?"

He crouched and pulled the revolver from the holster of the helpless man. Then rested the muzzles of both weapons against the caps of the bent knees.

"Zeke!" Oscar Taggart moaned and took a step forward as the injured man was made rigid by terror.

"Stay back, Dad!"

The owner of the Big-T swung his anguished face toward the half-breed. "You going to let a boy do your dirty work for you?" he challenged.

95

"I'm not a boy, damnit!" Zeke yelled. "I'm twenty-nine, Dad! And it's about time you realized that!"

"Old enough to know his own mind, I figure," Edge pointed out evenly, and ambled over to where the grim-faced younger Taggart was crouched beside the pain-wracked, fear-tensed man.

"They're Taggart cattle raised on Taggart money!" Zeke rasped. "And it's about time Dad and me did more than watch for stragglers."

"Not me who's giving you an argument, feller," the half-breed said, and dropped down onto his haunches on the other side of the helpless man. "Just concerned I gave him a choice."

He reached out and gripped one of Zeke's wrists to move it so that one of the Colts was pressed against the man's shirt front—left of center.

"A wrong word and you empty that gun into his leg. And we leave him here. If he says what we want to hear, one bullet in the heart will be enough." He showed a humorless grin to the doomed man. "Matter of whether he stays or remains."

"Zeke, don't do it!"

"Shut up, Dad!"

"Where did Saxby hire you, feller?"

The man's lips moved, but he uttered no sound. His complexion was sallow and he seemed to have become gaunter by the moment as he suffered the twin torments of agony and fear. His pants cuff and shirtfront were saturated with blood, which continued to seep from both wounds.

"Water," he managed to whisper after stretched seconds.

"Worst thing to give a man with a bullet in his guts," Edge told him.

Zeke was watching the half-breed eagerly, still determined to squeeze one of the triggers. His father was

96

held rigid in the grip of horror. Pancho eyed the brutal tableau with melanchoic resignation.

"I'm . . . I'm gonna die . . . anyway."

"That's the long and the short of it, feller. San Antonio?"

"Yeah, you . . . you bastard!" He got power into the profanity. But it caused a heavy drain from his diminishing strength.

"Just the three of you?"

"For now," the man answered, screwing his eyes tight shut as the words emerged, barely audible. "Just to hold you up for a while. Until Boyd Ash and his boys . . . boys get to town."

"Real tough bunch, uh, feller?"

He snapped open his eyes to direct depthless scorn up at the impassive half-breed. "If you was one of that bunch and I was your best friend, you wouldn't waste a bullet on me."

"Obliged," Edge said, and pointed to Zeke's left hand holding the Colt against the man's chest.

"No, son!"

The revolver cracked and bucked. The smell of burnt fabric was almost as strong as exploded powder. The corpse spasmed once and was still. Oscar Taggart sagged against the side of the chuck wagon. Pancho crossed himself. Edge straightened and Zeke stayed down on his haunches, sighing as he holstered his own gun. Then he looked up at the half-breed.

"Do you know anything about this man Ash and his gang?" he asked, and there was just a tic along his jawline to show he felt something after the killing.

"You heard what he said, feller. They wouldn't waste a bullet to put a best friend out of his agony. Figure that makes them real mean."

Chapter Eight

IT WAS impossible to tell exactly how many steers were lost during the frenetic stampede of the spooked herd. But no more than a hundred, Barney Tait guessed, after he made an experienced estimate when the cattle finally stumbled to an exhausted halt in a draw five miles north of their starting point.

He was mad at the *vaqueros* but he did not bawl them out, aware there had been no drovers to spare for side runs in pursuit of breakaways. But his anger found an outlet in a snarling row with Zeke Taggart—the foreman wanting to hold up the drive while the strays were rounded up and the boss's son demanding they be written off.

Oscar Taggart was a sullenly dejected and apparently disinterested observer of the quarrel. Pancho moved among his weary fellow countrymen, huddled in the makeshift camp close to sleep or riding line guard, reporting on the killings and checking on which of the group was now a stiffening pulp of trampled flesh back down the trail. Edge smoked a cigarette and silently awaited the inevitable outcome of the bad tempered disagreement.

And, at sun-up the following day, he resumed his role of scout when the slightly depleted herd was stirred from bed ground to continue the long trek northward.

It was another arid Texas day of blistering heat and

stinging dust, seemingly designed to make even more volatile the dangerous mixture of moods affecting the men in close contact with the massive herd of long-horns.

The tobacco-chewing Tait was more surly than usual, angered by the loss of the cows he was convinced should have been rounded up.

Zeke was relishing the pride of a swollen ego now than an explosion of violence had snatched him out from under the influence of his father.

The elder Taggart was disenchanted, having discovered that toughness in office-bound business dealings did not necessarily mean that a man had what it took to run his own affairs in the outside world. And in realizing this, he was not comforted by the knowledge that his son could so easily assume command. Rather, he detested this aspect of Zeke's character that he had previously never known existed.

With the exception of the gravely self-possessed Pancho, the Mexicans veered between grief for their dead *compadre* and anger with three targets—themselves for allowing their position to come about, the Americans they rode with for inviting the situation, and Matt Saxby for his single-minded purpose that had triggered the chain-reaction of danger and death.

But, as this day ran its grueling course—and many more followed the same pattern of routine work across country where nature was the only enemy—time and the necessity to handle the problems of the present dimmed memories of the past and blunted responses to what had happened in the south.

And only during infrequent respites in the exhausting pace of the forward push toward distant Laramie did the drovers have time to consider the implications of the half-breed's job with the Big-T. This would be at night when he rested in a shallow sleep under his blankets, one hand fisted around the frame of his Winchester; or at a brief water stop in the daytime when he might be spotted riding far out from the herd—ahead, to the rear, or at the sides. A lone figure on a hostile landscape whose sole purpose was to seek danger from a source more selective than the terrain and elements of nature. At such times, when a man was held briefly between sleeping and waking in the night or allowed his bloodshot eyes to wander away from the drinking herd in the day, he might respond to the sight of Edge in one of many ways.

Some resented him because of the extra money he was being paid while not having to do any of the back-breaking, muscle-aching, sweat-chafing work of riding herd on the steers. Others were contemptuous of him—recalling how he handled his personal trouble with Edwards in a way that caused him no harm, yet had failed to deal with the men who started the stampede until after a Big-T hand had died. A few were reminded that the half-breed was a symbol of new violence that had been promised.

But then Tait would order the drive forward again and Edge and the reason for his presence would be forgotten amid the heat and the dust and the flies and the stink of almost five thousand head of longhorns on the move.

The drive was a day east of the Pecos when the half-breed justified Oscar Taggart's decision to hire him. The early hours were cold and moonless, with a sky that was blanketed with low cloud. There was a half-hearted threat of rain in the chill air, lessening by the minute as he completed a wide circle of the bedded-down herd. He was a half mile south of the night camp, leading the gelding among a scattering of boulders at the base of a low bluff, when he smelled tobacco smoke in the damp air.

He came to an instant halt and the horse, familiar with the ways of its owner, was immediately as unmoving as the man. And remained still and silent when the reins were lowered to the ground.

A mumbled word had given Edge a bearing on where the smoker was positioned and he paused only a moment to slide the Winchester from its boot before he stepped away from the horse. Not directly toward the cluster of rocks where the word had sounded, but in a wide arc to take best advantage of cover.

A bottle clinked against metal and a man cursed. Another spoke placating words that were indistinct.

Edge, his bristled features set in a mild frown that did not even hint at the intensity of his concentration, closed in silently on his objective.

The rockfall, which had collapsed the bluff, had been a violent one, scattering the sandstone boulders across a broad area of grassland. The two, or perhaps more, men were positioned a hundred and fifty feet from the base of the rugged cliff, at a vantage point that allowed them an uninterrupted view of the herd, the night guards and the drovers who rested between the dying fire and the parked chuck wagon.

As the half-breed stepped between two heaps of boulders and saw the pair of hobbled stallions, his frown faded and he curled back his lips to display an icy smile. The men had not been watching the camp ground for long. Or else they would have seen him riding his circuit and been on their guard against his approach.

The two horses eyed him with brief indifference and returned to cropping at the dew wet grass between the debris of the rockfall. Edge trod as lightly as before on the moist, sound-deadening ground. The smell of strong tobacco smoke became more pungent. He heard the gurgle of liquor passing down a man's throat.

Another man growled. "Sight of all that beef's makin' me mighty hungry, Ellis."

"You been eatin' dust for three days, Hayes," the

101

other answered, and giggled. "Same as me. Take a drink to wash it down, why don't you?"

"On account of one of us has gotta stay sober to keep Boyd from blowin' our heads off, goddamnit!"

"Up Boyd's asshole!" Ellis snarled. "For givin' us this crummy job in the first place."

"Freeze!" Edge rasped. "Or for you fellers this could be the last place."

Ellis was in the process of snatching a cigar from his teeth and raising a bottle to his pouted lips. Hayes was peering down the long, gentle slope toward the herd. Both were seated crosslegged on the ground, Hayes between two boulders and Ellis at the side so that the glow of his cigar could not be seen from below. They snapped their heads around at the first word spoken by the half-breed. And the shock on their faces became more deeply etched as each additional word was built into the threat.

Hayes went for his holstered gun as he threw himself to the side.

Edge was a dozen feet away, seemingly as solid and incapable of movement as the pile of rocks beside him. The Winchester was canted to his left shoulder and he ignored it in his counter to Hayes's move. He drew, cocked and fired the Remington sixgun, moving only his right arm and hand. In the confident knowledge that there was no need to turn sideways on and thus present less of a target to the man trying to kill him. For Hayes was experiencing uncontrolled fear—the kind that triggers reckless haste instead of thoughtful speed.

And Hayes died while his Colt muzzle was six feet away from alignment with his kill. Taking the bullet through the center of his forehead on a downward trajectory that drove it behind his left eye and lodged it like an ugly mole projecting through the flesh of his cheek.

"You killed him!" Ellis accused as the Remington was cocked and swung a fraction of an inch to cover him.

"His choice, feller," Edge replied against a distant barrage of fearful shouting from the night camp beside the quiet herd. "Figure he was more scared of Boyd Ash than me. How d'you feel about that?"

Ellis was about twenty-five, made old before his time by liquor—his complexion a mottled red and his belly hanging over his gunbelt. He shook his head, struggling to complete the sobering up process started by the gunshot and its effect. Then he swallowed hard. "My old man always used to say where there's life there's hope, mister."

He suddenly realized the situation looked worse as he sobered. So he hurled away his half-smoked cigar and unbuckled his gunbelt one-handed while he raised the bottle to his lips and attempted to suck comfort from its neck.

It was quiet again down at the night camp, as the first gray fingers of approaching dawn stretched across the cloud above the eastern horizon. Then, as Ellis got unsteadily to his feet, leaving his gunbelt on the ground, two riders began to gallop up toward the scattered rocks spread out from the base of the bluff.

Ellis looked ruefully at the empty bottle of rye, then down at his dead partner and across at Edge.

"He also tell you nobody ever finds the answer to anything in a bottle, feller?" the half-breed asked.

"Maybe, mister. I never listened to him much." Another gulp of pre-dawn air. "I guess you wanna know what Boyd has in mind, uh?"

A nod as the half-breed stepped away from the heap of rocks to close in on the overweight, drink-sodden Ellis.

"Then you'll kill me?"

"No, feller. Then I'll kill Ash."

103

"What about me?"

"Only kill you if you don't tell the truth."

The unwashed and unshaven face of the drunk crinkled as he considered this. "How'll you know, mister?"

The two riders from the night camp skidded their mounts to a half in front of the rocks Ellis and Hayes had used for cover.

"Yet another killing, *señor?*" Luis Lacalle rasped through the gaps in his teeth.

"Him or me," Edge answered without looking away from Ellis. "If me, then maybe you next."

Zeke Taggart swung down from his saddle to stand beside the Mexican. But his expression was deadpan in contrast to Lacalle's grim-faced sourness.

"Just the two of them?" he growled.

"Here," the half-breed confirmed.

The prisoner's fear had expanded since Taggart and the *vaquero* moved in among the rocks. Both men were bleary-eyed from too much work and not enough sleep. And their weariness sounded in their voices. But they wore guns and in the dirty gray light of a cloudy dawn the anxious Ellis drew only a fleeting impression of them. To him they were just two more armed captors. The American was tall and thin, the Mexican short and broad, with equally unkempt appearances. And Ellis saw only their hardness.

When Zeke halted in front of him, Ellis flinched away. But not far enough to escape the upswing of a folded knee into his crotch.

"Sonofabitch!" the pained man groaned and dropped hard to his knees, both hands clawing at the base of his belly.

Lacallè rasped a curse in his native tongue, then lunged toward Taggart. But Edge was closer and had merely to swing his right arm and extend it out and up to press the muzzle of the Remington against a pulsing

104

temple. The younger Taggart became immobile, both hands clenched into a single fist he had intended to smash into Ellis's pain-contorted face.

"What the hell?"

"You're a late developer, Zeke," the half-breed muttered. "But it ain't right another feller should have your growing pains."

Ellis went down onto all fours and scuttled painfully away from in front of where Taggart was held in a rigid stance. But there was no possibility of escape and no opportunity for retaliation. Agony was piled on fear to increase his helplessness.

"Jesus, you were happy enough to have me kill a man the other day," Zeke complained.

"No, feller. You were happy. I didn't give a shit one way or the other. Best you go down the hill and help get the cows moving."

"What's the frigging difference with this man?" Zeke snarled in reply.

"He didn't try to kill me, is all."

Zeke was trying to control the pulse, which expanded and contracted the flesh of his temple under the pressure of the Remington muzzle. But he could not. "And you wouldn't dare pull that trigger against me!" he challenged. There was a note akin to childish triumph in his voice as he swung his head away.

Then he screamed. The sound in perfect unison with the crack of a bullet from the revolver barrel. His flesh was seared black by the exploding powder and blood oozed in a crimson line—along a shallow furrow across the side of his head. Just above his right ear.

Shock and pain drained the strength out of him and he collapsed into an untidy heap. But he did not lose consciousness. He raised a hand to the superficial wound and almost choked on an indrawn breath when he saw the blood on his fingertips. When he looked up,

105

it was to see Edge pushing the still smoking gun back into its holster.

Then his gaze was trapped by the hooded eyes of the half-breed, which in the first light of day had never looked so blue or so hard between their slitted lids. Each was as thin and dangerous as the honed edge of the razor he carried.

"Listen, feller," the tall, lean, brown-skinned man said, his thin lips hardly moving in front of his clenched teeth. "Your pa's paying me to keep trouble away from his cows. Barney Tait's along because he knows the cows and the quickest way to get them to Laramie. Lacalle and his buddies are the best drovers Tait was able to hire. Pancho's a good cook. Your pa's our guarantee that we're all going to get paid."

"Not any more you frigging won't!" Zeke snarled and scrambled to his feet. "When he hears what you just did to me, he'll fire you faster than you can blink. After all, I am . . ."

He was holding his blood-stained fingers to the wound, which was already beginning to dry up.

"Oh yeah," Edge interrupted. "I almost forgot about you. But that's easy done, Zeke. You're an irritation. An itch. And I just scratched you."

Chapter Nine

EDGE and his prisoner started out ahead of the herd and widened the gap with every mile they covered during the day. Ellis rode behind the half-breed, his stallion forced to follow the gelding by the lead line which linked the two horses. The line was a length of Ellis's lariat. Other lengths had been used to lash his feet to the stirrups and his wrists to the saddlehorn.

At midday, Edge shoved pieces of jerked beef into his mouth and held his canteen while he drank. For the rest of the time he ignored him and Ellis quickly learned the futility of complaint. And as the horses carried their silent riders closer to the Pecos so the prisoner's hatred for his captor grew more intense.

First there had been a degree of gratitude for Edge's calling a halt to the beating. Then the pain of the first and only blow that was struck. Discomfort at having to be constantly in the saddle with little opportunity to shift his posture. Thirst for the unopened bottle of rye whiskey in his saddlebag. Fear of Boyd Ash who was waiting with at least seven other men, as evil as himself, at the Pecos crossing. Finally the hatred that, as it expanded, served to calm the fear that was liable to swell into a mindless terror.

The half-breed was also experiencing a brand of enmity as he rode across the dusty country under the gray sky, the humidity pasting his clothing to his flesh and sending sweat runnels through the dirt and bristles on his face. But his disaffection was directed inwardly; its basis the new-found knowledge of a facet of his character he had previously been unaware of, a flaw in his make-up that was both detestable and dangerous.

This was that he could be affected by an event and yet not be conscious of any change within himself.

It had happened before. Long ago, during the War Between the States when, at the height of the bloodiest battles, he had been gripped by a kind of brutal exhilaration—was driven to slaughter the enemy with the momentum of a temporary but deep-rooted madness.

But each episode of this kind had taught him a lesson so that, when he found Jamie's mutilated body on the Iowa farm, the need to kill—although stronger than it had ever been before—was subject to self-control.

Similarly, when he set out on the long search for the Sioux brave he was certain had taken Beth from their Dakotas homestead, there was a solid purpose for his murderous mission.

Perhaps there had been other occasions during his violence-ridden life when a degree of madness had charted his actions. But since his experiences of the war, he had always been aware of his objectives—however vaguely—when he caused injury or death to his fellow man.

Until Oscar Taggart had offered him this job on the dusty street of the nameless Mexican town across the Rio Grande. And he had accepted for a counterfeit reason.

"You bastard, Edge!" Ellis croaked, as his stallion pulled up short behind the abruptly halted gelding.

"No sweat, feller," the half-breed replied evenly. "I ain't so touchy in that area any more."

The liquor-dissipated man astride the stallion had no way of knowing what Edge meant. And had no inclination to find out. For, like the half-breed, his attention

108

was held by the men on the far bank of the Pecos River.

It was late afternoon now, the sky still low and leaden with dark clouds, which continued to hold back on their threat of cooling rain. Edge had halted his mount four hundred feet short of the east bank of the shallow, smooth running river, in the insecure cover of a stand of sycamores. Immediately ahead was an expense of low brush that extended to the water. Then the three-hundred-feet-wide river. On the opposite bank the ground rose more steeply and the vegetation was sparse. But boulders, niches in the slope and rock outcrops provided solid cover.

Leading to and away from each bank there was a broad, trampled strip on which only tufts of yellow grass grew, a rough trail fashioned by the passage of cattle herds, which had been driven across the Pecos at this point. A half mile to the south the river cut through a ravine. Northward it curved from sight around a shoulder of rocky hill on the west bank, perhaps a mile away.

Directly across the river from where Edge and Ellis were halted in the timber beside the cattle trail, eight men were in full sight. Men in their thirties and forties, dressed for riding and fighting. Unshaven and travel-stained. Weary from riding and impatient for fighting. Four of them squatting on the river bank, playing poker with pebbles for their stakes. Four more sitting on the ground with their backs against boulders. One of these chain-smoking ready-made cigarettes, another reading a dime novel, two others apparently sleeping. But not sleeping. For, like the rest, this pair cast constant glances out across the rippling, gurgling river. And, on each filthy and bristled face that was swung so frequently toward the east, Edge and Ellis could read the bad-humored eagerness for action that belied the men's relaxed attitudes.

109

"But you use any word louder than a whisper, it won't be your hand that gets a hole in it."

Again, the hapless Ellis could not understand the half-breed's cryptic comment. But the threat was plain enough.

"I told it like it is," he rasped miserably, licking dry lips as he continued to gaze hopelessly across the river.

Edge nodded in acknowledgment. The situation was precisely as Ellis had said it would be. Matt Saxby had deposited two and a half thousand dollars of hard-earned cowhands' money in a San Antonio bank and made it known that he was looking for guns to hire. When the Ash bunch rode into town, three hundred dollars had already been withdrawn—a half payment for the trio of gunslingers sent to delay the Big-T drive.

Now there was just eleven hundred dollars in Saxby's San Antonio bank account. For Boyd Ash had the other eleven hundred, with a promise of a like amount after he had halted the Big-T drive. Nothing had been said about the possibility of the first three gunslingers returning to claim their second half payment for services rendered.

Ellis's story had checked out thus far. The presence of the Ash bunch on the other side of the Pecos was further proof that he had been too scared to lie when he blurted out answers to the half-breed's questions, across the crumpled corpse of his partner in the strengthening light of this morning's dawn.

Ellis had revealed that he and Hayes were sent to confirm Saxby's claim that the Big-T herd was being moved north by just a handful of *vaqueros*, a trail boss, the owner and his son, and a single gunman. He added that after making the check, the two were to ride west and report to Ash at the Pecos crossing.

"So now you know I told you the truth, Edge," Ellis whispered hoarsely. "I'm as stiff as a friggin' board and thirsty as all get out. You told me I'd be okay if I didn't try to sell you any bill of goods."

"You come to any harm so far, feller?"

The half-breed unhitched the lead line from around his saddlehorn and tied it to a low branch of the nearest sycamore.

Ellis watched him with baleful eyes. "I ain't so far away from dyin' of fright, goddamnit."

"I turn you loose now, I'll maybe die of something else."

"One against eight, for chrissake. You ain't got a chance. Not against the Ash bunch. Turn me loose and I swear I'll . . ."

"Easy, feller. Which one's Ash?"

Ellis ran his tongue along both lips. "The one's that's smokin'. Okay, there ain't no reason you should trust me, Edge. But there's a bottle in my saddlebag. The one down on the left. Give me a drink, at least."

"Don't want you sitting tight that way," the half-breed answered, and eased down from the saddle.

He hitched his gelding to the same branch as the stallion and slid the Winchester from the boot.

"What if you don't make it?" Ellis groaned.

"You worry too much, feller."

"What d'you expect?"

"The worst. That way I'm never disappointed."

He moved away from the helpless Ellis then, going south through the timber and brush toward the ravine. Thinking that his final flippant comment to his prisoner contained more than a grain of truth.

Ever since he had been made aware that his ruling fate decreed he was to possess nothing that he desired, he had almost always taken what he wanted with the certain belief that it would be snatched from his grasp. So it was possible he had suffered more than a man who expected to keep that for which he fought. For was not the pleasure of having diminished by the knowledge that soon it would be lost?

And was this final awareness of the depth of his destiny's cruelty the reason he had held back from taking Isabella, when he could have done so on countless occasions? But even for his negative attitude toward her, he had been made to pay the price. Without knowing what it was until he saw Ezekiel Taggart smash a knee into the crotch of a defenseless man.

When he witnessed this brutal and cowardly act, Edge saw a mirror image of himself that was only slightly distorted. Zeke, free from a sheltered existence under the dominant influence of a father whose power had been abruptly diminished, had felt the need to flex his newly discovered muscle.

The half-breed had been sure of his own power since the early days of the war. But for a long time—between his first meeting with Isabella and the moment when he drew against the Quintero brothers—part of the kind of man he had become was in a state of suspended animation.

Since then?

Had he tried, he could have handled the two Mexican cattlemen without need to kill them. His treatment of the elderly couple who ran the dry goods store had been triggered simply by spite. Likewise the act of crippling a man's hand because of misused words.

Killing Hayes this morning and the shootings after the cattle stampede could not be included in the catalogue of uncharacteristic acts he had committed or condoned since taking the job Oscar Taggart offered him. Those men died for the good reason that they had had it in mind to kill him.

Everything else?

A reaction to the slaughter of Isabella Montez. She had been his for the taking and he had failed to claim her because he was afraid of the consequences when he would eventually lose her. But she had died anyway, caught up in the wash of violence that marked his progress along every trail.

And he had thought he was empty of emotion with which to mourn her passing. But he had been wrong. Somewhere deep inside him there was a response that had been secretly nurtured on the long ride from San Parral to the village on the bank of the Rio Grande. And not until he saw Zeke Taggart lash out at Ellis did the half-breed realize what it was.

Deep into the ravine, he crossed the Pecos River, treading carefully to find a solid footing in the soft bed and holding his Remington and Winchester high above his head. At one point the water flowed around his shoulders and the current threatened to snatch his legs from under him. But a new-found strength of purpose powered him toward the opposite bank without mishap. And he was effortlessly and instinctively cautious as he headed north in his dripping wet clothes, as eager for violent action as the eight men he intended to kill.

He veered away from the river, moving diagonally up the slope to gain a high vantage point above the waiting Ash bunch.

As he crouched in a niche behind a small outcrop with leafy brush to either side, he was conscious of the memory of Isabella, which he had sub-consciously ignored for so long, and embittered by her loss to him. But not as a woman—or even a person. Simply as a possession he had failed to use.

But he could relegate this callous thought to the dark recesses at the back of his mind as he raked his narrow-eyed gaze over the unchanged scene seventy-five feet below and away from him. For she and all that had happened—and not happened—between them were a part of the past. And he had at last assimilated the teachings of their lesson.

He shot the chain-smoking Boyd Ash first, blasting a bullet into his heart as he lit a fresh cigarette from the butt of the old one. The bullet that twisted through his body thrust him hard against the rock at his back. Then he folded forward and became inert, head and arms limp between his splayed legs.

Two of the card players died before the leader of the bunch was still. One took a blood-gushing bullet in the head and the other was hit in the heart with a shot that drilled through his back. Both were stopped in the act of powering up from the ground, turning, and drawing their Colts.

The five survivors of the initial burst of fire from the half-breed's rifle screamed and cursed and blasted wild shots as the pair of new corpses thudded their unfeeling flesh to the ground.

Isabella had nothing to do with the dead and living men below the ruthless killer on the rocky slope. For he was no longer a disoriented wanderer grasping the first opportunity to vent vicious spite at the slightest provocation—against whoever it happened to be for no reason he understood.

That phase was gone.

And, if he felt anything, briefly, as he exploded a fourth bullet to spin another card player into blood-pumping death, it was a mild sense of regret about two other corpses.

He killed a fifth man before the remaining trio gained the solid cover of rocks. It was another back shot, fired with the same total lack of compunction as the one that had hit the card player. The man was running away from Edge, seeking cover. The bullet took him low down, smashing through his spine. Its impact added momentum to the run and he did not halt until he pitched face down into the shallows at the river bank. He thrashed his arms, making white water to contrast with the red of billowing blood. But he could

114

not get his face above the surface and within moments became a sodden, drifting corpse.

Three Winchesters sent a hail of lead toward the half-breed's position and he crouched low to feed fresh shells through the loading gate of his own rifle.

The men below him had died, and would die, because it was their paid assignment to stop the Big-T herd. And it was Edge's paid assignment to get the longhorns to Laramie. That was reason enough to slaughter them and to risk his own life against their defense. But a man's actions always had some premise on past experience and the half-breed's strength of purpose and will to succeed in this instance was augmented by the deaths of two cowhands. An American named Edwards and a Mexican he could put no name to.

Risking ricochets, he bellied out of the niche. To backtrack on the route he had taken up the slope, making use of the same cover as before. And he did this unseen, having chosen his initial position because of its escape route.

Each man below emptied his Winchester and hurried to reload. Then they realized the attacker was no longer pouring a lethal hail of bullets down the slope.

"Wes?"

"Yeah?"

"I think we killed the bushwhackin' sonofabitch!"

"You wanna go up and check on that, Jim?"

"I sure as hell ain't gonna."

Edge bellied down the slope, a yard or so at a time with a halt in between. He had seen where Wes, Jim and the third survivor of the Ash bunch had scrambled into cover. Now he kept a constant check on them to insure they did not change positions.

"I reckon he could be waitin' us out, Chas! Jesus, he shoots good!"

"And hears good, too, you dummy! Keep the talk down, the both of you!"

There were stretched seconds of silence. Then the rasping sounds of whispered words scratched the riverside stillness of early evening.

Because he was the kind of man he had been forced to become, Edge could not live by any socially acceptable code. But he had always striven to maintain an ethical standard that raised him a cut above such men as those who rode as the Boyd Ash bunch—no matter how narrow that cut. Thus he experienced the mild regret that he, a professional gunman, had humiliated a cowhand into trying to kill him. And the nameless *vaquero* who was pulped into the ground many miles back down the trail? Regret, with perhaps a feeling of failure. For the half-breed was paid to keep trouble away from the herd and he had neglected his job while still unknowingly under the influence of an event a thousand and more miles away.

But now there was no such side issue as he made his way back to the ravine and recrossed the river. All was quiet on the west bank at the cattle-crossing point in the gathering dusk under the gray sky, which looked low enough to reach up and touch.

"Figure you're dying to say something, feller," he rasped to the tense and shocked Ellis as he came up to him in the stand of sycamores. "If you do, you'll be one over the eight for the last time."

Ellis screwed his eyes tight shut and nodded curtly. When he opened them again, the half-breed was gone, having dropped down onto his belly to ease out through the brush between the timber and the river. Jim, Wes and Chas were in full sight, crouched tensely at rocks that protected them not at all from the advancing enemy. They were silent and unmoving, prepared to out-wait the man they thought was above them, or perhaps simply waiting for the cover of night.

116

At the bank of the river. Edge went up on one knee. He pressed the stockplate of the Winchester against his shoulder and took aim at the closest target. His lips were curled back from his teeth and his hooded eyes were narrowed. He was exposed now, and afraid of death. But there was no element of bravado in his actions. He had to show himself to allow for the swing of the rifle needed to cover each target.

He squeezed the trigger and harnessed his fear to increase his speed. One man died from a bullet that entered his side to find his heart. Two more yelled their panicked fear and whirled to aim their rifles as Edge pumped the lever action of his. The man who had won most pebbles in the card game was hit in the belly and knocked over backward.

A wild shot cracked across the river, loosed by a trembling man aware that he was the final survivor of his group. The bullet went over Edge's head as the half-breed jacked another shell into the breech. And Ellis shrieked his terror as the lead smashed through the sycamores.

"No!" the last man left of the Ash bunch screamed, fumbling to work the lever action of his repeater.

His voice sounded simultaneously with the report of Edge's rifle. And he died with a crimson stain spreading across his shirtfront and tears streaming down his face.

"Your boss should have told Saxby that, feller," the half-breed muttered as he came erect, feeling the tension drain out of him.

He scanned the corpses littering the opposite bank with no sense of triumph. He merely vented a low sigh of satisfaction at a job well done as he turned his back on the scene and went to where Ellis sat on the stallion, slumped in the saddle from the after effects of the mind bending tension.

"You massacred them!" the prisoner croaked, star-

117

ing with horror-wide eyes at Edge as the half-breed slid the Winchester into its boot.

"What did they plan to do to the Big-T outfit, feller?" Edge countered without interest in the answer, as he approached Ellis and drew the razor from the neck pouch.

The man astride the horse became tense again, then almost collapsed with relief when he realized the restraining ropes were to be cut.

"What?" was the only word he managed to force from his constricted throat as Edge finished slicing through the ropes.

"On your way, feller."

Ellis licked his lips and blinked. "You mean it? You won't kill me if I leave?"

Edge took the makings from his shirt pocket and grimaced at the mess of wet tobacco and papers. "My word is about all I ever get to keep," he muttered.

Ellis made to heel his stallion forward, but paused. He looked down at Edge as the first spots of rain dropped from the evening sky.

"There's money in the pockets of them dead men, mister. And eight horses over there that'll fetch good prices in El Paso or someplace like that. You mind if I help myself?"

"You won't get none from me."

Ellis swallowed hard. "Thanks a lot."

"Pleasure's all yours."

The young gunman rode away from the timber, out onto the cattle trail and splashed across the ford. He had the bottle out of his saddlebag and up-ended to his mouth before he was halfway to the far bank.

Edge dug an oilskin cape from his bedroll and donned it before sitting down on a tree root to gaze impassively through the lightly falling rain.

Ellis worked fast and furtively at robbing the dead, with frequent swigs from his bottle, and he pointedly avoided looking back across the river. When he was through he led his horse up to the top of the slope and out of sight over the brow. A few minutes later the unmoving half-breed heard the beat of many hooves as the man led his four-footed spoils away at a gallop.

Then, for a long time, there was just the hiss and splatter of falling rain hitting the river, the earth, the rock, the vegetation, the living man and the dead ones. The clouds broke up later, and rolled eastward to reveal the bright dots of stars and allow the moonlight to shaft down on the scene of carnage. The night air grew colder and Edge exchanged the oilskin cape for a thick, warm, knee-length coat.

When he heard the distant thud of the herd's hooves against the rain-softened ground he mounted the rested gelding and heeled him out onto the trampled trail, which was now a strip of sucking mud.

Barney Tait and Luis Lacalle came into sight first, riding at point to either side of the lead steer. Both men made as if to rein in their mounts when they saw the stationary rider on one side of the river and the deathly still forms sprawled on the opposite bank. But then the foreman snapped an order and both he and the *vaquero* angled into the path of the longhorns' leader—to halt this steer and the thousands stretched out behind.

After the rain, the cows were unexcited by the smell of the Pecos and were content to graze quietly on the damp grass either side of the trail.

Then the tobacco chewing Tait growled another order to Lacalle, which sent the *vaquero* reluctantly back to report to the Taggarts. Only weariness was visible on the bristled face of the stockily built foreman as he walked his horse down to where Edge waited.

"That the Ash bunch?" he asked with a cursory nod across the river.

"It was."

119

"The man you had told the truth, uh?"

"His life depended on it."

Tait came close to showing a smile. "Fine. You did a good job, Edge."

"No sweat."

"We'll bed the critters down on this side tonight. Take 'em across in the mornin'."

"Figure you know your job, feller."

Tait wheeled his horse and the half-breed rode back to the head of the herd with him. Then he watched with mild interest as the American trail boss and the *vaqueros* closed up the longhorns into a tighter bunch until his attention was captured by two horsemen curving around the cattle toward him.

The two Taggarts—Zeke with a dirty, wet, blood-stained bandage around his head—halted their horses with a smooth, newly learned skill. They stared down at the stiff and sodden corpses. Both were trail weary, but that and the family name were all they shared now. The father was like an older, smaller, skinnier imitation of the man who had started out from the Big-T Ranch. The shallowness of his expression as he attempted to display the depth of his shock was an indication of how much his strength had been drained. Whereas it was obvious that Zeke had been further hardened mentally and toughened physically by the passing of another day. But still there was a childish quality about the way he accused:

"You want to hog all the glory for yourself, Edge?"

"Ain't no glory in killing people, feller," the half-breed replied. "Was earning my pay, is all."

"It is not a part of your job to almost kill Ezekiel," Oscar Taggart croaked.

"No sweat," Edge answered. "I won't make an extra charge for that."

Zeke stoked his hatred for the half-breed as his father attempted but failed to generate anger in response

120

to the cynicism. He jerked a thumb down toward the sprawled dead and grimaced as he asked, "The man who led you here is among them?"

"No."

"You turned him loose?" Zeke snarled.

"We owed him."

"But he was one of Ash's men, frig it!" Zeke snapped his head around to survey the moon shadowed country. "He could . . ."

"He's gone, feller," Edge assured evenly, and grinned bitterly with his mouth. "Kinda like the sun at the end of a bright day."

"What?" Zeke growled absently, still afraid of the night-shrouded Texas terrain on all sides.

"Heading for El Paso with a bottle of rye whiskey for company. By now I figure he's stinking in the west."

Chapter Ten

THERE was no more rain as the Big-T drive pushed on, swinging northwest after crossing the Pecos to pass over the foothills of the Sacramento Mountains. And no hint of further trouble paid for with Saxby's donated money.

Barney Tait continued to set a cracking pace due north through the Territory of New Mexico, crossing the trickling stream that was the upper reaches of the Pecos, the Cimarron Cut-Off and the Santa Fé Trail to reach Colorado Territory.

The closer the herd moved to Laramie, the less disgruntled with their lot the Mexicans became. Their doubts of the past were forgotten as they relished the prospect of journey's end and the high reward that would be theirs when it was achieved. And with the danger of a surprise attack by hired guns apparently gone, they were able to concentrate wholeheartedly on their job.

There was even a quality of pride about them as they worked, or when they rested at the end of each exhausting day. For they were skilled trailherders aware they were doing a fine job against high odds. Tait never let up on bad-mouthing the *vaqueros* but his cursing demands for better than best no longer angered them, for they had come to accept that his ill-humor was a deep-rooted trait of the man's character. He was a cattleman who liked cows better than people, which was bad for the people working for him. But he knew his trade and the Mexicans who were in the same business could respect him for this.

Zeke also earned a degree of respect as, day by day, he shed some of his rich-man's-son ways to learn and develop skills that made him useful on the drive. But those who had the perception to see below the surface of the younger Taggart recognized that a complete transformation was impossible. For there was always an underlying superiority in Zeke's attitude, no matter what he was doing. He was in a situation for the first time in his life when material possessions and abstract status provided no support, where, if a man wanted to impose his will on others he had to be stronger, smarter and more skilled than the rest. So Zeke learned his lessons sullenly, resentful of the need to be taught. And with an ulterior motive.

Edge saw more of Oscar Taggart than of anyone else concerned with the drive, for the old man no longer pretended he was anything but a hindrance when he rode as drag behind the stinking, dust-raising, fly-infested herd. And he had taken to sharing the seat of the chuck wagon alongside Pancho, or accompanying the half-breed during his constant circling of the moving longhorns.

He seemed to physically shrink with each passing day, his face always pale behind the newly acquired tan, his green eyes dull, his sparse shoulders sprinkled with falling hair as well as dandruff. He looked sick and yet, the half-breed guessed, the man's constant expression of distress had less to do with his physical suffering than his mental misery.

He spoke little for many of the long, hot days he rode beside Edge, and this was not simply because the half-breed failed to encourage conversation—if that had been what he wanted Taggart would have chosen to spend more time aboard the chuck wagon. For

Pancho's mood had improved ahead of the *vaqueros* as the drive progressed and the fat, mustached cook allied happiness with garrulousness.

But Oscar Taggart was comfortable with the taciturn Edge.

They were north of Pueblo in central Colorado in the lee of the Continental Divide, toward the end of another hot, trouble-free day when the broken old man made a comment that required more than a simple word or gesture of accord or disagreement from the half-breed.

"Ezekiel's going to turn out a harder man than I ever thought I was, Edge."

"Seem to recall you saying the idea of this trip was to shake him out of whatever he was, feller."

Taggart sighed, gazing vacantly into the northern distance while Edge continued to maintain an easy surveillance in every direction.

"It was, and when we came west I couldn't have hoped for anything better than what he's become. But all the mistakes a man makes start out as thoughts in his head."

"You've changed, too, uh?"

"You know it." He sighed. "I've made a great deal of money in my life. Without once getting my hands dirty, having my back ache or feeling the need to vomit from looking at a dead man spilling his life's blood."

"I ain't no expert on cattle drives," Edge answered. "But I figure they can't all be like this one."

Taggart waved a hand in front of his face, as if swatting a fly. "Only thing I'm an expert at is reading reports and balance sheets and giving orders. But I've always known there's nothing easy about ranching in the cattle business. On the range or the trail it's hard and it's dirty and it's dangerous. The same with coal mining and railroad building."

"For every man who dies in those businesses, a lot

more make a living out of them," Edge contributed flatly.

"I'm not looking for excuses!" Taggart said sharply.

"You're talking to the wrong man if you are, feller. Stating a fact, is all."

The old man was silent for a long time. Then, unconcerned by Edge's disinterest in the conversation, he continued to promote it. "I'm an expert on facts, Edge. The kind that are supplied to me on clean, crisp sheets of paper, which I read sitting in a comfortable chair behind a polished desk in a safe office. Bald facts concerned with men working their butts off long hours for low pay to swell the Taggart fortune. Almost every week there's one fact concerned with the death of a worker. Sometimes a group of workers: a mine cave-in, a boiler explosion or a ranch accident. Most of them would have been avoidable if more money had been spent on renewing worn-out equipment or there were a larger payroll to stop men from working so long and so hard they become potential victims of fatal mistakes."

"I fought a war that had something to do with abolishing slavery," Edge growled and drew a sidelong glance from Taggart as the old man realized he had ignited a spark of angry interest deep inside the half-breed.

"What does that have to do with . . ."

"Nobody's forced to work for you, feller," Edge answered, his voice still taut.

"You are wrong," Taggart countered. "You saw the situation in south Texas where there are more men than jobs. It's the same in Kentucky where the Taggart coal mines are sunk. And in Mississippi, Alabama and Georgia where another Taggart enterprise is building railroads. Men are glad to have a job, however low the pay."

"Nobody's forced to work for you," the half-breed

125

repeated, his tone even again. "A free man can always leave and go someplace else."

"Not if he has roots! Not if he has just the one skill which is of no use to an employer elsewhere! Not if he has the responsibilities of a wife and family!" It was Taggart who was moved to anger now.

"A man ain't a tree, feller—he can cut his roots without dying. If he learned one trade he can learn another. And if he wasn't sure he could provide for them, he ought never to have raised a family."

The old man seemed about to snarl an enraged contradiction to the half-breed's placidly spoken argument. But then he lost the tense rigidity and returned to his vacant contemplation of the rugged terrain spread northward. His tone became as miserable as his appearance.

"You're a man of fixed ideas, Edge. And the strength to live by them. So was I until this trip, but it's changed me. I'm convinced for the better. Whereas Ezekiel is being changed for the worse. And he'll be a far more dangerous man than you are. Because the Taggart Corporation is vast and he'll ride herd on its interests far harder than I ever have. Even though he'll know the kind of suffering this will inflict on his fellow men."

"What are you trying to say, Mr. Taggart?" the half-breed asked evenly. "That you wished I'd killed him instead of grazing him?"

The old man was shocked, his strangely wan but tanned face twisting into a distorted replica of human features. "You're not making a sick joke are you?" he gasped.

"I'm not doing anything except filling in my end of a conversation you started," Edge answered.

The dusk was gathering and Edge had veered his gelding to the side and slowed the pace, allowing the herd and drovers to pass so that he could make a final

126

circle before Tait called halt at a suitable bedding ground.

"I don't like what he's turning out to be," Taggart rasped. "But he's my son and he's shaping into what I was before I came west. And if you harm him again I'll spend every cent of Taggart money, if that's what it takes, to make you pay."

"No sweat, feller," Edge responded to the threat. "Only way he'll bother me is if he tries to stop this herd getting to Laramie. And I guess he's got a better reason than anyone else to get the Big-T cows to the stockyard."

Taggart was still angry. But he brought himself under control. "If we reach Laramie before the deadline we'll get a much better than market price for the cattle. If we don't, there'll still be a profit. That extra margin looked fine on paper. Right now it seems I'm the only man who doesn't think it's worth it."

"Right now you're still the boss," the half-breed pointed out, but his tone and a brief expression interrupting his impassive face revealed his lack of conviction.

"In theory only, as you well know," Taggart accused. "It was my plan to hand over control to Ezekiel when we reached Laramie. But for all practical purposes he has that now. And this worries me considerably."

Edge had been rolling a cigarette. He struck a match to light the tobacco and drawled, "We're finally getting to the point?"

The old man chewed on his lower lip for a few moments. "There's going to be more trouble from Saxby. I don't have to tell you that, I guess?"

Edge spat a flake of tobacco off his tongue. "That do-gooder's two and a half grand into Laredo cowpunchers. And he's already spent more than half of it. If he ain't gonna be more unpopular than you in

127

south Texas he had to make good or make it known he tried everything."

Taggart nodded. "That is my view exactly. And it is my intention to see that nobody else suffers from whatever Matt Saxby plans as his next move. In short, I intend to accede to whatever demands he makes."

He eyed Edge as if he expected surprise or even shock to be registered on the lean, hawklike face of the half-breed. They were in back of the herd now, covered with dust pasted to their features by the afternoon's sweat not yet dried by the cooling air of evening.

Edge spat some dirty saliva from his mouth. "And you figure that even if Saxby sits still to listen, Zeke won't talk your new language?"

"Would you back down if this beef was yours?"

They had swung around behind the men riding drag and the chuck wagon and started forward again, alongside the strung-out herd of longhorns.

"Mine, yours or your son's, feller," Edge answered, rasping between teeth clenched on his cigarette, "the cows don't make any difference. Way I figure it, reformers who ain't willing to stand up and fight for what they want changed are shit on the asshole of the lousy world."

Taggart grimaced. "Like Ezekiel, you regard Saxby and the men who support him with contempt. I should have known it was futile to talk to you."

"I had a lot more respect for the men who started the stampede and for the Ash bunch, Mr. Taggart."

"Highly paid gunslingers like yourself!" The old man's voice was vicious with a bitter scorn of his own.

"On account of the law of supply and demand," Edge answered as, far ahead, Barney Tait moved into the path of the lead steer and the herd began to bunch and halt. "If there were too many men like me around, I'd move on or I'd do something else."

"What if there was nothing or nowhere else?" Taggart rasped. "Human rights is not a matter so simple as you try to make out."

Edge flicked away his cigarette. "Ain't no such thing as human rights, feller. Just human privileges. And if I figured I wasn't getting as much as I'd earned, I'd do my own fighting."

"You think I'm like Saxby? Well, I'm not."

The half-breed showed his teeth in a cold grin as the final light of day was swallowed up by the western horizon. "That's your privilege, bought and paid for. And that's why it ain't a waste of time you talking to me, Mr. Taggart. You hired me and I figure you're still the boss. You want to give in to Saxby and the rest of them fellers waiting for paid guns to win for them, it ain't no skin off my hide."

"A hundred and fifty dollars a week is a cheap price to pay for a man's principles, Mr. Edge," Taggart muttered, still scornful.

The half-breed shook his head. "Now the ownership of the herd makes a difference, feller," he said quietly. "If this beef was mine, I'd kill any man who even stepped in their way on the trail to Laramie. Mostly when a man dies, he fills his pants with crap. I'd scoop that all up and take it back to Texas. Then I'd tip it over those cowhands. So folks could see what they are. No, Mr. Taggart, it ain't my principles you bought. Just my loyalty."

The old man considered this in silence for perhaps a full minute. Then nodded, perhaps in acknowledgment of the half-breed's reply, or to signal a personal conclusion he was sure about. "Then you would not obey an order by Zeke that you knew countermanded my wish?" He cleared his throat. "Even though you might agree with what he tells you?"

"One of my privileges I got is to pick who I work
129

for, feller. And right now I'm working for the man who owns the Big-T herd."

"Thank you. I'll give Pancho a hand with getting dinner ready."

Both men had halted their mounts beside the herd. As he spoke, Taggart wheeled his horse and clucked him into movement, back to where the Mexican cook was unhitching the chuck wagon team from the traces. Edge heeled his gelding in the opposite direction, to complete his watchful circuit, and met up with Zeke Taggart who was one of the drovers assigned the first watch of herd riding.

"For a man who doesn't talk a lot, you've sure been having a lot to say to Dad," the man on the white stallion said, a quizzical look in his red-rimmed, green eyes. The bandage had been off his head for several days now and the healing scar of the bullet's furrow served to emphasize his recently acquired toughness.

"He's got a problem."

Zeke sneered. "And you care?"

Edge shrugged. "He's bought my time at a high price. He didn't say anything to make me want to quit."

The younger Taggart was irritated by the half-breed's close-mouthed attitude and made another attempt to needle him. "Since the slaughter at the Pecos River you haven't earned a cent of what you're getting paid."

Edge sighed. "You could be right, feller. But that's your pa's fault."

Zeke scowled his confusion. "What?"

"My job's to keep trouble away from the Big-T herd. Yet he's just told me I ain't allowed to kill you."

Zeke became rigid in the saddle, at once both angry and afraid. "You and he have been discussing me?" he snarled. Aware he would learn nothing from Edge, he gazed furiously across the backs of the herd toward the

130

chuck wagon as the flames of a cooking fire leapt from kindling.

"Yeah, we talked a lot of crap," the half-breed allowed.

Zeke snapped his head around, his anger rising at the taunt. But he knew Edge well enough to distrust the dead-pan expression and nonchalant attitude of the man astride the gelding. And frustration caused by fear triggered another childish response from the younger Taggart.

"You think you're such a big shot, don't you, mister?"

"No, feller. Straight and fast is all."

Zeke jerked on his reins to turn the white stallion away from Edge. "One day you'll meet your match!" he sneered.

The half-breed nodded. "I guess Lucifer's ready and waiting for somebody to strike lucky."

Chapter Eleven

"You want to kill me now?" Edge asked evenly. "Or take a chance on not being fast enough later?"

The tall, blond and handsome Matt Saxby sat on his horse with a Winchester at his shoulder aimed at the quiet-spoken, unmoving half-breed. There were more than twenty cowhands stretched out on one side of him. As many on the other. They also had their repeating rifles out of the boots but held them angled across their chests, not threatening the lone rider who had come to a halt, thirty feet in front of them.

It was early morning in southeast Wyoming Territory, just a day away from Laramie. The clear air was still cool from the night, the sun a weak and watery yellow disc filtering its light and warmth through thin cloud.

The men aligned across the trail and flanking pasture land had been in sight for many miles as Edge rode toward them, his gelding moving at an easy pace on a loose rein. For this section of the Wyoming plains was as flat as a well-laid floor, its only prominent features widely scattered stands of cottonwood trees. It was as he followed the trail's curve around the most extensive clump of timber for many miles that he first saw them—like a line of dark stakes driven into the verdant land.

Had it not been for the conversation with Oscar Taggart in central Colorado the half-breed might not

132

have continued his unhurried progress along the trail. But his new orders had been plain enough and they had not been countermanded following the furious quarrel between the father and son at the night camp north of Pueblo.

So Edge rode on, certain of only two things about the stakelike forms which materialized into the figures of men astride horses as he drew closer: that there were too many of them to be hired guns and that their overt presence signaled a desire to avoid a violent confrontation.

Nobody said anything until Edge halted his gelding, raked his gaze along the entire line and then fixed his glinting eyes on Saxby to issue the menacing invitation.

"We don't want anyone else killed, Edge," the man replied, as calm as the half-breed.

Some of his allies sat in their saddles easily, with composed expressions and relaxed muscles. Others were nervously tense as they surveyed the recently bathed and shaved man astride the travel-weary gelding, perhaps recognizing the latent evil in him or maybe simply recalling what Saxby had told them about him. A few exuded aggression, resenting his arrogance in the face of such impossible odds.

All the men were cast from the same mold as those who had ridden over the hill behind the Big-T ranch house on the day before the drive north began. Young to middle-aged, strongly built for their trade and weathered by exposure to the elements. They sat tough cow ponies laden with the tools necessary to those who worked with cattle. Their rifles were mostly 73 Winchesters, their holstered handguns Frontier Colts. They were the kind of men who would kill in self-defense or for a cause in which they believed. It was unlikely that any one of them was a killer by instinct.

Saxby certainly was not. He had pumped the action of his rifle and leveled it toward the target while Edge was still two hundred feet away. But in such a situation as this the Winchester was merely a symbol of his authority rather than an instrument of death.

"You changed your mind, too?" the half-breed said, draping both his hands over his saddlehorn.

"Too?" Saxby was perplexed.

"Taggart. The old man. He figures he's been wrong for a long time."

"How many men had to die to make him see that?" Saxby was genuinely interested.

"All you sent, feller. Minus one. A *vaquero* and one of your buddies from Laredo."

"What you mean, mister?" a solidly built, squint-eyed cowhand in his forties called from the line. "About the boss of the Big-T changin' his mind?"

"Who's asking?"

Saxby spoke first, his aim still rock steady to keep the rifle muzzle trained on Edge's chest, left of center. "Names aren't important. These are cowhands from all over. Denver, Greeley, Cheyenne, Laramie. Couple from Dodge City even. Three from Abilene. Some have worked for the Big-T. Most for outfits that pay almost as badly as Oscar Taggart."

"That eleven hundred dollars you had left must be spread pretty thin, feller," Edge drawled with a slow look along the line.

"No cash, mister!" Saxby growled with sudden anger. "I guess that must be hard for a man like you to understand. These men are just ready to fight the Big-T to set an example."

"I asked what you meant, mister!" the squint-eyed man demanded.

"Taggart is ready to give Saxby what he wants," Edge supplied.

"In a friggin' pig's eye!" a gray-bearded man snarled. "Not as easy as that! I reckon this guy's tryin' to trick us!"

134

"It ain't being called a liar that bothers me, feller," Edge said to the man with the beard. "But I already told this do-gooder I'd kill him if he pointed a gun at me."

The half-breed was still sure of himself. The men were suspicious of him, but there was no physical evidence of danger, nor could there be a surprise attack on such open terrain.

"Let's not be hasty," the bearded man was placated by a man with eye glasses next to him. "I reckon we oughta hear what his boss has to say before we start any rough stuff."

"Yeah, that's what I say!" another man agreed. "We got nothin' to lose by waitin' for Taggart to show up with the herd."

Several other voices were raised in assent.

"Come to think of it," the bearded man growled when the noise subsided, "there ain't a lot else we friggin' well can do."

"So put up the rifle, Matt," the bespectacled cowhand advised. "The Big-T outfit sees us with a gun on their man, they'll maybe figure we plan to make a fight of it."

"Obliged, feller," Edge muttered, and drew, cocked and triggered his Remington.

There were two periods of shocked silence so intense they seemed to have a palpable presence in the cool, bright air of the Wyoming morning. The initial reaction of the men lasted for less than a second—as Matt Saxby started a sigh and began to swing the threat of the Winchester away from the half-breed. And Edge's right hand streaked to his holstered revolver, leveled, and fired it.

Then came the report of the exploded powder, a tiny sound on the vastness of the plain, but almost deafeningly loud in the ears of men who stared in horror at the killer. Which still beat against their drums in memory as they snapped their heads around to see the victim.

The bullet took Matt Saxby in the heart and it was on his handsome features that horror was most deeply etched, as he lived for part of a second and then tipped backward out of his saddle. His left foot slid from the stirrup, but his right was trapped in the *tapadero* until his falling weight tore it free and he thudded into an inert heap on the center of the trail.

Only the sounds of his fall scratched the second, longer period of shocked silence after the shot.

Then men gasped, groaned and cursed. And Edge experienced an ice-cold fear of death as all eyes returned to him. It was not a new sensation and he had endured it so many times he was able to remain outwardly composed to all who looked at him. In fact, the men's shock was deepened by the total lack of change in him. His Remington was back in its holster and both his hands were draped over the saddlehorn. It was as if nothing had happened—that there was no blood seeping corpse crumpled on the ground at a midway point along the line of mounted men.

"It was personal," the glinting-eyed, narrow-lipped, dark-skinned man said.

"You friggin' killed him!" the squint-eyed man accused, his voice a croak.

He, like most of the others, had made to level his rifle at Edge. But stayed the move when he saw the revolver had been holstered.

A nod. "When a man holds a gun on me while he chews the fat, there's always a cover charge, feller. He paid."

"But . . ."

Edge was still aware of ice-cold fear at the pit of his stomach. He moved his hands slowly to insure his actions could not be misinterpreted by nervous eyes, lifting the reins from the saddlehorn and tugging them to one side as he touched his heels to the flanks of his mount.

"Other folks' business," he said as the gelding turned. "His and mine. You fellers want to get in on that kind of trade, I guess I'm through."

He put his back to them as the hooves of his horse disturbed the signs of his approach on the trail. His fear had lessened now, for his judgment of the men as a group had been correct. Had they been expecting such cold-blooded murder, they would have gunned him down without a qualm in instinctive defense of one of their own. But their shock in response to his brutality had lasted too long; and any man who blasted him after that would have been fully aware of what he was doing. And here the size of the group was to Edge's advantage. On his own, any individual in the line might have acted impulsively to trigger a shot to avenge Saxby's death. But no one was on his own and they all used up more time in self-conscious consideration of what the others might feel.

By then it was too late, for Edge had his broad back to them, which was the ultimate deterrent against being shot by men whose code extended far beyond the simple bounds of keeping a promise—for good or ill.

"Hey! Hey, you! What about Taggart?"

The half-breed did not turn his head. "I'll tell him you're here. What happens then is your business. And his."

There was a muttering behind him, but that was all. No crash of a rifle shot to sooth for all time the nagging itch which attacked his skin between his shoulder blades.

Then the lead steer wandered out of the draw to the south and showed at the side of the cottonwood grove. Two riders appeared next, followed by the first group of longhorns in back of their leader.

"Hold up, mister!"

Edge recognized the harsh voice of the bearded man and he reined in his horse. And turned just his head to look back at the cowhands. The earlier low-toned talk had achieved something—the election of a news spokesman now that Saxby had been silenced for ever. All the men were holding their rifles in the same manner as when the half-breed had first closed in on them.

"You want something?"

"Yeah! Whatever it was Taggart was gonna give Saxby! You tell him that!"

"I already said you won't get no argument from him."

There were still some anxious faces in the line. But not so many as before. Now, most of the group were infected with a brand of grim determination.

"We got no reason to believe what you say, mister!"

Edge pursed his lips. "A man can only learn by experience, feller. Saxby took his lesson to heart the hard way."

He faced front again and heeled his horse forward.

The two point riders kept the herd moving at a steady pace along the trail and grassland spread out on either side, and did not angle in to halt the lead animal until Edge was only yards away. The riders were Tait and Lacalle who divided their nervous attention between the half-breed and the line of riflemen who had begun to advance on the stalled herd.

"He got a whole friggin' army now?" the Big-T foreman growled, unmindful of the familiar irritation of flies winging across his bristled face.

"Saxby ain't got anything any more," Edge answered, looking along the strung out and grazing herd.

Almost five thousand head of longhorn steers that for the first time since they left the Big-T ranch were being ignored by their drovers. For, like Tait and Lacalle, the *vaqueros*, Zeke Taggart, and Oscar Taggart and Pancho aboard the chuck wagon were exclusively concerned with the half-breed and the line of riders moving inexorably across the plain at his back.

"He's dead?" Tait rasped.

"You kill him, *señor?*" Lacalle asked.

"It was his decision," Edge answered, watching at long range another quarrel between the two Taggarts as the father climbed down off the chuck wagon and unhitched his horse from the rear.

"Just now?" Tait demanded and waved a hand toward the approaching riflemen. "With all those guys around?"

"It was personal. In that kind of shoot out three's a crowd. That many's an audience."

"You are very sure of yourself, *señor,*" Lacalle growled.

"It comes and goes," Edge answered, as Oscar Taggart started to gallop alongside the grazing herd, leaving his angry son at the rear. "It's been coming good since the day before we crossed the Pecos."

There was no more talk between the trio as Taggart raced toward the front of the herd from one direction and the line of rifle-toting cowhands rode toward the same point at an unhurried pace.

Above the opposing groups anxious for a peaceful end to the death drive from Texas, the sun remained pale yellow behind the filtering effect of the streaky, dirty white clouds. The air was still and cool. But men sweated, the stink of the steers masking human odors. To the north, the crumpled body of Matt Saxby looked like a pile of something dark on the distant yellow trail.

The forty or so cowhands brought their mounts to a halt in a straggled line fifty feet away from where Edge, Tait and Lacalle were grouped.

Oscar Taggart slowed his mount and sucked in deep breaths of morning-cool air.

"Who are they?" he gasped.

"Men who want to talk your language," Edge replied.

"Not hired guns?" His anxious green eyes were searching the line for a familiar face.

"Hired hands is all."

"Saxby?"

"Gone to heaven or hell. Like all of us, I figure he's got friends in both places."

"If you're Taggart," the bearded man yelled, "it's us you're supposed to be yakkin' to."

The old man stared quizzically at Edge for a full second more. Then scowled his dissatisfaction and heeled his stallion out across the intervening ground between the head of the herd and the line of impatient cowhands. There were no signs of nervousness in their attitudes now. Some even grinned their confidence as they surveyed the trail-weary drovers, small in number, who would be the enemy in the event of trouble.

"You men can put away your rifles!" Oscar Taggart opened as he halted his stallion and swung his head from side to side to sweep his eyes over every face. With his mind made up and in the grip of a determination to have his way, he no longer looked so exhausted and gaunt. His voice was strong. "The killing is all done and I'm here to tell you that those who gave their lives did not die in vain.

"I understood Matthew Saxby was among them and I regret that most deeply. Because it was his ideas and actions that forced me to see the error of my ways. So I'm fully aware of what he wanted, not for himself as such, but for men like you. And I intend to insure that his ideals will be realized. Not only as regards pay and conditions for the Big-T outfit and other Taggart operations. I shall also exert whatever influence I have on my business colleagues in many areas of trade and commerce to . . ."

A rifle shot exploded. Then another. And another.

Not loud sounds to the ears of the men at the head of the herd because the reports came from far off, but awesome because each man knew what would follow the fusillade.

Perhaps there were more shots but, if there were, the sounds were masked by the thunder of many thousand hooves against the Wyoming grassland.

The massive herd lunged into a stampede as a single unit, horned heads down the hides stretched taut over bone and muscle as natural instinct drove each steer away from the cause of its panic.

For long moments there was no ordained leader of the fear-crazed animals as those at the rear—closest to the cracking rifle—began the charge. These slammed into the longhorns in front of them and thus was the terror transmitted through the herd.

In the space of three fast-fired rifle shots the entire Big-T herd was charging forward, intent on nothing except headlong speed that blinded every animal to any obstacles in its path.

"Stupid sonofabitchin' little shit!" Barney Tait roared as he wheeled his horse and drew his Colt.

Luis Lacalle cursed once in his native tongue as he performed the same actions as the trail boss.

Oscar Taggart had time only to look back over his shoulder and express an aging frown of despair before his mount was panicked by the thunder of hooves and the vibration of the ground. His horse bolted.

The line of American cowhands was as fast as the *vaqueros* to respond to the stampede, commanding their horses with reins and spurs as they drew their revolvers.

Edge experienced a mixture of cold fear and angry uselessness. Then, as his gelding signaled a move to panic into a bolt, he responded positively.

Gunfire crackled and his gelding was more attuned to this sound than were the two ponies of men whose

141

business was cattle. Perhaps the animal beneath the half-breed was even comforted to some extent by the familiar roar of guns. But whether this was so or not, the rider regained control of his mount, using the speed of the bolt but commanding its direction.

And Edge was carried across the front of the first wave of charging longhorns on a diagonal line, retreating from a danger that others knew better than him how to handle.

Oscar Taggart's life depended upon sheer luck for good or ill. With neither the youthful strength nor the skill to impose his will on the bolting stallion, he could do nothing except try to stay in the saddle as the horse was gripped by the same blind panic as the steers. And had the animal galloped straight ahead or swerved to the right, the old man would have survived.

But something in the terrified brain of the stallion dictated a turn to the left. And that was the direction in which the enraged but coolly working cowhands had elected to swing the herd, taking their cue from the cursing Barney Tait.

The turn had already been made by the time Edge had ridden clear of the stampede, brought his gelding to a skidding halt and wheeled him.

Tait's Colt had exploded first, sending a bullet high into the clear morning air. Lacalle was just part of a second later in firing his revolver. Tait matched the shot with a hand signal, which *vaqueros* and American cowmen alike recognized and acted upon. And many spurred their mounts into hurried but ordered movement while others held their positions and exploded their handguns skyward.

Thus the massive herd, which had been triggered by gunfire from a docile standstill into a terrified charge, was veered to one side by another barrage from a different direction.

Every man saw Oscar Taggart fall to inevitable

142

death, but none was in a position to witness what happened after he had been shaken free of his racing mount. Nor to hear the thud and snap of his dying as unfeeling hooves burst open his flesh and cracked his bones.

His mouth was gaping wide as he toppled sideways from his saddle, screaming in terror, rage or frustration. And perhaps it was this shrill sound which drew a response from the stallion, this or the abrupt shedding of a rider. Whichever, the big horse swerved to the right and was suddenly a lone animal racing across open country with nothing to fear but the memory of a danger that no longer existed.

For the Big-T herd galloped straight on its newly ordered course, in the wake of the big steer that had been the leader all the way from the home range, flanked by fast riding cowhands who yelled at the tops of their voices and exploded countless shots into the air.

Edge sat his saddle and stroked the neck of his gelding, speaking softly into one pricked ear of the animal. But the horse continued to tremble, eyes bulging and nostrils flaring, until the ground beneath its pawing hooves was still—the stampeding longhorns, and the riders content to let the herd run itself into exhaustion, thundering away to the west.

Then the horse was calm and at ease again and the half-breed heeled him into a gentle walk over to what was left of Oscar Taggart.

All of what once had been a man was there on the trampled grass and hoof-pitted earth of Wyoming. But it was no longer in one piece. For, after countless steers had crushed Taggart into a pulpy mess of crimson meat mixed with stark white bone fragments, others had torn the body apart and scattered it over a broad area. Thus was the verdant pasture land scarred

143

by a broad swath of moist red, featured with gruesome heaps of the trampled flesh of a human being.

The gelding was as unmoved by the sight and smell of recent death as was the man in the saddle. But the memory of terror was still freshly imprinted on the brain of the animal. And he was comforted by the soothing sound of Edge's soft spoken words.

"There's a cattleman who let his business get on top of him."

Chapter Twelve

FAR off to the west the herd was slowed by the dictates of failing stamina, and the men who had once been maneuvred into opposing forces continued to cooperate in turning the front runners back onto the center of the following stream of tiring longhorns.

The activity was so distant now that only the sound of gunfire would have carried to where Edge rode slowly in on the stalled chuck wagon and mounted man beside it. But guns were no longer necessary, the weary steers responding to the less powerful sounds of men's voices.

Pancho did not have a voice. Nor anything else possessed by a living man. He was slumped across the seat of the chuck wagon, a revolver still clutched in his right hand and a hole in the center of his forehead with a widening trail of dried blood leading down to his open right eye. The other eye was closed and the single open one seemed to be watching the approaching half-breed, showing mild displeasure.

Zeke Taggart's expression was more intense, his hard green eyes asking a question Edge refused to answer until it was put into words.

"Dad didn't move fast enough, did he?"

"He couldn't hold on long enough," the half-breed corrected, reining his horse to a halt six feet in front of where Taggart sat the white stallion. He jerked a thumb toward the dead Mexican cook. "Pancho try to stop you?"

"It was him or me, Edge. You understand that kind of situation."

The man's veneer of toughness was beginning to crack. He was still holding the Winchester with which he had started the stampede and killed Pancho. He was resting it across his middle, in a two-handed grip with the hammer back. His fists tightened around barrel and frame as his fear of the soft-spoken, dispassionate half-breed mounted.

"No sweat, feller. Unless your problems are mine. And that'll only be if you don't have any ready cash."

Zeke blinked.

"Your pa's dead," Edge augmented. "I guess that means you inherit the business. And the debts. I was paid just the one week in advance."

"Same as the Mexicans . . ." Zeke started to blurt.

"That's their business," the half-breed cut in.

Zeke nodded vigorously. "You'll get paid. Everyone will. Just as soon as the herd is handed over to the army in Laramie. There'll be plenty for everybody."

"After that?"

Nothing had changed about Edge's attitude, expression or tone of voice. But Zeke sat easier in his saddle now, as a group of riders headed out from the stalled herd toward the chuck wagon. The new owner of the Big-T was confident he would not be gunned down by the impassive half-breed.

"It'll be the same as it always was!" His tone was vehement and his newly bronzed face expressed spiteful determination. "Dad was getting soft. He was going to give in to the men, wasn't he?"

"Guess he must have told you what he planned, feller."

"Sure he did! And he also said he wasn't going to hand over control to me at Laramie the way he intend-

146

ed it to be at first. He was going to sell out to every man who works for us before he retired! All my life he tried to make me the same kind of a sonofabitch he was. And as soon as it happened he went soft!"

The three men who had ridden from the herd pulled up their horses ten feet from where Zeke Taggart and Edge faced each other. Barney Tait was at the center, flanked by the bearded man and Luis Lacalle. They had taken their time riding up, mounts and men recovering from the exertion of the chase. But the anger of the men simmered dangerously close to boiling point in back of their accusing eyes. The Mexicans did a double take at the slumped form of Pancho and curled back his lips from his gapped teeth in a scowl of hatred.

"It was Taggart or the cook," Edge said in Spanish.

"We all speak that language, too, mister!" the bearded man growled.

"I don't, Edge!" Zeke snarled, again gripping his Winchester tightly. "And with Dad dead you're working for me. Does everyone understand that?"

He was not afraid of the trio's enmity toward him. But neither were Tait, Lacalle and the bearded cowhand concerned by Zeke and Edge.

"You did okay," the tobacco chewing Tait said to the half-breed. "Out there when this crazy shit spooked the critters into a run. You got outta the way and let guys that know cows take care of it."

Edge nodded. "Like I always say, every man to his trade."

"Or business," the bearded man added. "And this ain't none of yours. Unless you want to join us."

"I ain't the joining kind, feller."

"Unless the price is high enough, señor," Lacalle rasped. "But your high price will not be paid on this occasion if you continue to . . ."

"He wanted his old man dead, Edge," Tait interrupted, his voice harsh with impatience. "The boss told me

147

that days ago and he wrote and signed a piece of paper. Assigns the Big-T spread and stock to me in the event of his death. So it'll be me gets paid for the herd at Laramie."

He grinned his pleasure at this and tobacco juice squeezed between his clenched, discolored teeth and ran down the bristled jaw.

"So best you just sit and watch, mister!" the bearded man growled. "If you wanna get paid by the only man who'll have cash at Laramie. Unless, like I already said, you wanna help us make Taggart pay. For puttin' our lives on the line as well as his old man's?"

"Edge!" Zeke croaked, the old fear constricting his throat and forcing his hands into tight fists around the rifle. "You can't . . ."

He snapped his head around from staring at the un-moving half-breed—his eyes widening in terror at the sounds and scene of a trio of men drawing guns on him.

He gasped and tried to bring his Winchester to the aim.

But there was not time.

A single gun was jerked from its holster and ex-ploded six times in rapid succession, the trigger finger constantly pulled back as the gun hand swung one way and then the other, the free hand fanning the hammer.

The bearded man, Tait and Lacalle each took a bul-let in the chest. Then the curses and screams they vented as they began to topple from their saddles were silenced by other bullets. And blood torrented from head wounds, in contrast to the slow spreading stains on the fronts of their shirts. The riderless horses snorted and scratched at the ground as the limp forms of the corpses crashed down among them.

"God in heaven, thanks," Zeke blurted. "For a second there I thought you were with them."

"I'm with me," Edge answered flatly, turning the

148

Remington skyward and clicking the cylinder around to let the expended shell cases drop from the chambers. "Until somebody pays me to be with them. Right now I'm being paid Taggart money."

"But Tait said Dad has assigned . . ."

"And I guess he wasn't lying," Edge allowed, taking bullets from his gunbelt and feeding them into the empty, smoke-smelling chambers of the Remington. "But it ain't like it was a couple of steers that were transferred from one owner to another. Proving that piece of paper's valid would take a lot of legal time and trouble. A man could starve waiting."

Zeke grimaced. "So you killed three men just to save time. Irrespective of the rights and wrongs of it?"

Edge showed a cold grin as he holstered the fully loaded revolver, recalling Oscar Taggart's ambivalence toward necessary killing. "If your pa hadn't changed, Zeke, he'd have been real proud of you. Seems you've become almost exactly what he used to be."

"And I'm proud of it! Even if I had to kill him to show what I am!"

Edge spat to the side. Then nodded as he dug the makings from a shirt pocket. "Like that almost as much as your money, feller."

Zeke was perplexed. "What? That I killed my father?"

The half-breed's lean, bronzed, narrow-eyed face expressed a brief scowl. "That you decided to do something and went right ahead and did it. Without needing to have a bunch of two-legged sheep to back you."

He struck a match on the stock of the Winchester jutting out of the boot, lit his cigarette and tossed the match down onto the corpse of Tait. The flame was out before the stick of wood lodged on the blood-stained shirt.

"Or even two," he growled.

Taggart was still uncomprehending, unaware of the

149

complete loner's ruthless contempt for men like his father, Matt Saxby, Barney Tait, Luis Lacalle, Boyd Ash and even, except in this one instance, Zeke himself. Equally for men who took no drastic actions unless they were led by others. Like a herd of Texas longhorns and the lead steer.

After long seconds, the new owner of the Taggart empire abandoned his attempt to understand and shifted his puzzled gaze toward the grazing herd where the Mexican and American cowhands were waiting.

"You think they'll do what I tell them?" he asked, his eyes and tone apprehensive.

"You're the boss, feller," the half-breed answered. "And right now they haven't got anybody to tell them what to do."

Zeke Taggart wasn't convinced as Edge turned his horse and started toward the herd. He hurried to catch up with the half-breed. "We should reach town by nightfall. For one day I'll pay double rates. That should keep them happy. You'll make sure nobody gets out of line?"

"You're the big wheel now," Edge muttered. "You make sure they know that. I guess they'll figure out for themselves that I'm around to make sure nobody mistakes what you mean."

Zeke licked his lips and scowled, as if he didn't like the taste of the salt sweat of fear which had dried on them. He looked out across the pasture land toward the ghastly stain and small heaps of human flesh that had once been his father. "I'm not sure I didn't make the biggest mistake of anybody," he croaked. "I'm already starting to hate myself for what I did."

"Learn by it, feller," the half-breed growled, the bitterness of his tone directed at himself. "Maybe that way you won't screw up again."

"That's what I intend."

"You and me both." He curled back his lips to re-

150

veal his teeth in a humorless grin. "And maybe tonight the whole town will love us."

"What?"

"I hear tell Laramie welcomes careful drovers."

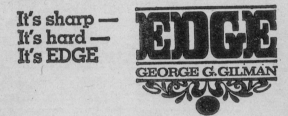